Tears Of A Masterpiece

Written By Tequila Barksdale

First Edition: November 2020

Tears Of A Masterpiece/Tequila Barksdale

ISBN: 978-1-943616-36-7

Cover Art by Jeremy Fields

Publisher: MAWMedia Group, LLC
Los Angeles | Reno | Nashville

DEDICATED to Mary Barksdale, my beautiful mother and super-woman; a woman who embodies strength, courage, and resiliency.

Table of Contents

Chapter 1: What a Dream

Ms. Strong, you have a call on line one; it is the contractor. He would like to speak with you about the new Boutique. He says they are almost finished, and he would like you to come and do a walkthrough to determine if your vision is coming to life. "Wow, great, I am excited"! My second store is finally about to open; please transfer him to my line....

It was the morning of graduation, and my family had made it into town the night before. There was a beam of sunlight that hit my face, followed by a woman loud enough to wake the neighborhood. My mother, Evelyn, entered my bedroom yelling, "Jahiri, get your butt up girl before you are late for your own graduation". My mother's facial expression revealed excitement, satisfaction, and joy, knowing that in a few hours, her youngest would be receiving her Master's in Business. I jumped up as if I were a little girl throwing myself into my mom's arms; overwhelmed with joy and excitement. I gave her the biggest hug and kiss.

"Jahiri, get up, girl!!" I could hear Eve screaming from the living room as she was approaching my room, "Ma, is she up?!" Sitting in my mom's lap with a big smile on my face, I yell back at her, "girl, why are you so loud?" Eve "It's not every day that you get to witness your only little sister graduate from school with her MBA; it's kind of a big deal, especially when you had that breakdown in undergrad, and we all thought you were dropping out of school." As she stood there talking about how we are going to celebrate tonight, she did her interpretation of "twerking" which made me glad she was a doctor. Mom couldn't stop laughing at Eve, who made it even funnier to me. My mom got up, saying, "I hope that's not how you are going to dance when you go out embarrassing folks." Smiling, Eve responded, "Ma, now you know I got my moves from you." My mom now looking back and forth at Eve and I with straight disgust on her face. "Child, don't blame me for not having rhythm." We all laughed hysterically because my mom, who appeared to be this beautiful innocent woman, could dance; I mean, dance her butt off. "So Jahiri, what are your plans now that you are finished with school? I do mean after we celebrate, of course?" "I'm gone make them big dollaz like you, Doc". Walking out the room laughing, Eve stated, "not talking like that, but I am glad you decided to get a business degree; it will provide you more sustainability than that design stuff you did during your undergraduate." As always, she cannot just give a compliment without her little side remarks, but today is my day, so I won't waste my energy.

Standing in the mirror preparing for graduation, I cannot believe that I actually made it. I was filled with excitement but nervous because I was finally finished with school and uncertain of what will come next. I had so many thoughts going through my mind, such as worrying if I don't get approved for a business loan, what if people don't like my designs, what if I fail as a business owner. A small kick at the door quickly interrupted my overthinking. It was Zarie kicking the door. "Auntie, I have to pee, can you hurry up in there?!" Laughing, I quickly finished getting dressed. As I walked into the living room, I could hear my father, brother-in-law, and my nephews rooting as if they were at a football game. My father, Jason, walked over and kissed me on the forehead "I am proud of you." No time for the emotional stuff, I grabbed my gown so we could head to the graduation ceremony.

"Hey, Bri," I yelled as I walked over to my best friend, Sabrina. I ran over and gave her a big hug as we both began to fix each other robes and hats then Bri stops and says "girrrrl, we are finally done with this shit" she has no filter what so ever. After helping each other get our gowns together, we both went our separate ways to go sit with our program.

Sabrina and I had been friends since the fourth grade, but when it was time to leave after high school, Sabrina decided that going away for college wasn't for her at the time. We maintained our friendship; however, there were times that it was tested. Sabrina took some courses back home, but she didn't finish. So in my senior year of undergraduate school, I decided that I wanted to go back to get my masters. Sabrina was looking for a new start, so I offered for her to move down and be my roommate while she got her undergraduate degree, and I got my MBA. She hesitated at first, but one night, she called me with so much anger and hurt in her voice telling me she wanted to move in with me. I didn't question her. I didn't know why she had a change of heart but I was happy to have my best friend move back near me like we were when we were kids. She never told me what happened that night she called, and I never pressured her about it and look at her now; she is getting her degree.

Sitting in the fully packed auditorium, Sabrina found her family in the crowd, sitting next to my family. She sent me a text letting me know where they were. We began waving and posing for pictures. After all of the long speeches and other colleges being called, I heard, "would the candidates receiving their Bachelors of Accounting, please stand". Sabrina stood and walked across the stage as I cheered for her in the crowd. Sabrina was brilliant in my eyes; she sometimes lacked the drive. I guess the first announcer had gotten tired because he switched with another professor. Walking towards the stage, I began to think of all the long nights working on papers, creating a business proposal, working two jobs, interning, missing time with family, and I began to cry. I never thought, as a youth, I would get one degree, but today, I was receiving my second degree. Then on the loud intercom, I heard a man with the very deep and loud voice announce Jahiri Strong, Magna Cum Laude. I walked across the stage, receiving my degree, and in the crowd, I could hear my family and friends screaming my name. The Dean had asked prior to the announcing of the student to keep the cheering at a minimum, but I never understood why when they knew for a fact that families were going to celebrate their children's accomplishments, and my family was no exception. My dad had a bull horn that I made my mom hide because that just would have been too much, even for me.

After all the students marched out of the auditorium, I began calling Eve to find out where they were so we could meet and take pictures. I saw Sabrina in the crowed talking to someone but was very far, and when I called her name, she didn't turn around, so I left to find my family. My mother Evelyn was gathering everyone together; Eve yelled, "Ma, this is like your 100th picture!" "I can take as many pictures as I want Eve, just shut up." About thirty minutes later, Sabina showed up asking if we had seen her family. "They were waiting, but since they could not reach you, they have gone to the hotel." Eve told her, "oh yeah, your mom said call her if you want them to go to dinner with you". She then pulled Sabrina to the side, "I saw Chris here, and I saw you talking to him after graduation. Why is he here?" "Oh, he had a frat brother that graduated today, and when he saw me, he called my name, so I went over and spoke." Eve giving her a puzzled look, "oh, okay. Well, congratulations, and I am proud of you." As I walked up on them, Eve was passing Sabrina a few cards from the family. "Thank you to everyone." Waving as she walked off. Shortly after Sabrina left, I left the school with my family to go to dinner for the continued celebration.

Chapter 2: Old Friend/New Friend

"Girl, I can't believe it has been three weeks after graduation." "I know right, time is just flying by. Pass me the tape, Sabrina." "I wish we would have thought to move out when all of our family was in town so that we could have more help." Sasha and Chrissy, two of my friends from college, said in unity, "well, what are we doing" while packing the kitchen items. "You two are being very helpful; that's not what I mean. It would have been quicker if we had more people, that's all I am saying," Sabrina replied. "Oh, okay, well, make yourself clear because we don't want to be where we are not being appreciated," Chrissy responded to Sabrina rolling her eyes. "Okay, ladies let's not start arguing today. I'm very thankful that you ladies have cleared your weekend to help us move."

Chrissy and Sabrina had been rivals since they met years ago during our freshman year. Sabrina did not care for Chrissy because she felt that she was taking her best friend from her. She told me the year she came down for homecoming that she got a bad vibe from her, but she never had valid examples of how, so I never entertained my best friend's jealousy. I was very open to making new friends and networking while in college, and I was not going to allow my childhood friend to take that experience from me. Over the years, I was glad that I didn't because Chrissy and I had become very close and considered her to be a very good friend more like my sister.

Sasha was finishing up her Ph.D. in college and I was in my sophomore year when we met, but we hit it off instantly. Sasha was hosting an event on becoming an entrepreneur, and I stopped by only because I needed a business event to attend for a class project. Sasha was intrigued by the type of questions and research that I had done prior to the event, so she introduced herself to me after the event. She instantly became a mentor, and even after she graduated, she would always provide guidance and linked me with events, people, and resources that would help me in furthering my career. After we gained a friendship, I eventually told her how I ended up at the event, but she said the reason behind me coming had nothing to do with how prepared I was for the event, which is what stuck out to her about me. I was all about women empowerment and was so grateful to have met so many people like Sasha that helped me through school. I joined a mentoring program that she started for individuals majoring in design or business. She even got me a job opportunity right after I completed my undergraduate degree at this design company owned by a Ms. Kelly, but I had just gotten offered another job as an entry-level art designer, which paid extremely more money and benefits, so I took it. I later found out that I was more so like a secretary and did nothing pertaining to design—not unless you count creating brochures for small events as design work. I should have taken my dad up on his offer to help me out until I find a career more so along the lines I wanted, but I didn't want to put that kind of pressure on my parents; I was a grown woman now, and I wanted to show them I could do it on my own or at least try to. When I went back to school, she was able to help me gain a part-time internship there, which I loved; however, the pay was little to nothing, but I knew I had made the right decision. I appreciated Sasha for being like a big sister and mentor to me; although, I would never take all of her advice because, just like my sister, she always thought she knew more. But unlike my sister, she would not get mad at me when I didn't do as she suggested. She always helped me out when she could or when something came up that she thought I would benefit from. Sasha was dope like that.

We were about finished packing when I asked, "would you ladies like to go to this Hibachi place they just built by the..."; before I could finish my question, Sabrina ran out of the room heading towards the bathroom. Chrissy asked, "what's her damn problem now, Hiri?" Shrugging my shoulders with a smirk on my face, "I have no clue; she can be really dramatic sometimes, or maybe she is trying to get out of packing." "Well, I wouldn't mind her leaving; she hasn't done anything but complain these past two days anyways. I just hope she is finished packing her things because they will be waiting on her when she returns." Chrissy said with a huge smile on her face as she gives Sasha a high five. I put a slight grin on my face; I always felt uncomfortable when people talked about Sabrina. But hell, she was right.

I loved Sabrina and felt like she was family, but I agreed with some of the things that people said about her, but I would never express it. Sabrina and I discussed her moving in with me while she finished up her undergraduate studies. Although we were the same age and had started college at the same time, Sabrina liked to party, and she flunked out after her sophomore year. She stayed out for almost two years and decided that she wanted to move to Atlanta with me as we planned when we were in high school. Needless to say, back then, everything was planned out so beautifully, but those plans didn't come to fruition.

Although that was not the case, I was excited about the thought of living around my best friend again but shortly after moving in together, I realized that things had changed so much. I realized that Sabrina was still fascinated by things that we were intrigued by as teens, and I did not know how to feel about that. Sabrina was supposed to help pay half of the bills but would lose her job because she said that she had too much work, and her classes were very hard. I felt that since I had some saving's I would help my friend. Although I hated my job, the pay was great. I could afford to help. Foolishly, I helped her by paying all of the bills the first year. Little did I know that it would be something that I do for the entire two years that we lived together. My family tried to warn me that the two of us living together would be a bad idea, so when this happened, I was too embarrassed to tell them about it. I just worked harder to keep up with the bills. It was extremely hard, but somehow, I made it. Funny thing, I use to come home to a dirty house, and I'd have to check myself. I was feeling like a tired and unappreciated husband thinking, *Damn this girl could at least clean.* She always had so many excuses and errands to run when I approached her about it. Shit, I don't know if I am happy that we were finished with school or just excited that we were finally moving into our own separate places. It is such a relief to finally have my own space and not feel responsible for taking care of another grown person. It feels like I have been freed from a toxic one-sided relationship.

"I'm ready," I stated as I entered the living room that was now filled with packed boxes. Chrissy and Sasha, who had recently finished changing, stood up, grabbing their bags and purses ready to go eat. Sabrina came out of her room half-dressed and said that she wasn't going to go for dinner because she wasn't feeling well, but she did thank the ladies for helping pack. The ladies told her to feel better and waved goodbye to her as they walked out the door. From the smiles on their face, I could tell that they were just happy she wasn't going out with us, but I didn't say a word.

After dinner, I went straight home because I had to prepare to move in the morning. When I entered the house, I went straight to Sabina's room; whose door was halfway open. I did not see her, so I yelled, "hey Bri, where are you?" No Response, so I called her on the phone. Sabrina didn't answer, but she instantly texted… "I started to feel better, so she ended up linking up with some friends for dinner, but I will be back either later tonight or early in the morning to move." I didn't mind; I just wanted to make sure she was okay, so I went to my room to take a shower and go to bed.

The next morning the movers arrived, and shortly after, Sabrina came home. She went to her room to change into tights and a t-shirt. Her friends came to help her move; she did not have as much as I did to move, so she did not get movers. She finished packing her things before I did, so she asked if we could speak to outside. Before I could get out the door, good Sabrina started talking.

"Jahiri, I would like to thank you for helping me so much for the past two years, girl; without your support, I may not have finished school; hell, let's be real, I wouldn't have."

"I love you sis, and if I had to do it again, I would, even though sometimes your crazy ass made it difficult." (thinking to myself, no I would never do this shit again)

"Well, I've been pondering for weeks on how to tell you this, but I could never figure out how; so, I am just going to come out and say it. I am pregnant, and I am moving back home to Illinois to be closer to family and the child's father."

"Wow, that's, that's surprising…I mean, congratulations, Sabrina. Why didn't you want to tell me? I mean, you have never had issues being blunt with me before. Your crazy ass is going to be a good mom; let's just hope it's not a girl, and she does you the way you did your mom growing up (laughing)."

"Thanks, girl, I wanted to tell you, but sometimes I don't know what to expect from you. I mean, you always have your shit together."

"Don't confuse working hard with having it all together because I don't; besides, you are a grown woman, and it's exciting to know that you are going to have me a niece or nephew. So, who is this guy? I didn't know you were dating anyone."

"Umm… well, he is a guy from back home you don't umm… know him like that."

"Oh, well, I hope to meet him soon. As long as you're happy and he takes care of you and the baby, I am happy for you."

"Well, we aren't together anymore; it was something that happened that shouldn't have, but you know how I feel about kids, so I am keeping my baby. He wasn't as excited, but he says he is going to be there for the baby."

Interrupting our conversation, one of Sabrina's rude ass friends yells from her candy red maxima, "hey Sabrina, we are ready to go?!" To this day, I still don't know her name, and she has been around a few times. Sabrina quickly hugged me and hurried eagerly to end the conversation by letting me know that she would call once she made it to Illinois and settled in. The entire conversation was strange, but I didn't have time to worry about that, so I went back into the house and continued to gather things as I waited for Isaiah to arrive.

Chapter 3: The New Guy

I met Chrissy in my freshman year. She was such a social butter-fly, but it was her confidence and determination that intrigued me. She knew going to college what she wanted to do, whereas I was studying to be an accountant because Eve felt it was a safe field for a promising future. Well, Chrissy became an Architect right after graduation, working with the company she interned for in her senior year, which resulted in her having a great career, financial sustainability, and a promising future. Chrissy was living the millennial college graduate dream, which is why Eve fell in love with her instantly; sometimes, I think she wanted her as a sister and not me, especially when I let the family know that I wanted to change my major to fashion design. You would have thought that I said I wanted to quit school altogether the way she overreacted. But Chrissy, she never judged me or pushed me to.play it safe she actually pushed me to use college to follow my dream and network; she was dope, and I loved her for that. She had the gift to capture people's attention and demand the floor with her conversations, which has landed her numerous projects all over the states over the years. When I hung out with her, we always had a good time.

Well, it was about a month after we graduated undergraduate school when Chrissy invited me to go to a party with her and she wouldn't let me say no to going out with her anyways being that she is rarely in town due to work. So, I told her I would be ready at 7 pm because I knew she would get there an hour early. At 6:15, the doorbell rings, and there was Chrissy with her hair in a flawless bun, makeup done as if she has a personal makeup artist, a pair of ripped jeans, sheer black and white striped top with a black bralette underneath that covered everything but her belly button, complimented with the black peep-toe heels that had the yellow bottom that I designed for her as my senior project. She always let me design things for her, and at first, I thought it was just to make me feel good until she would actually wear them out in public. She was really into fashion, so she knew how to rock anything that I made for her. It always made me feel proud of my work and grateful to have a friend that supports me.

On the way to the paint party, Chrissy explained to me that it was an event that some of her co-workers put together for another coworker who is having a baby and taking a year or two off of work. She said that they have this new guy who is from Los Angeles taking her place, so it's kind of a two in one combo farewell and welcome party for them.
She was still an intern. This should be fun. We danced all night.

When we arrived at the venue, we picked out our smocks, decide where we want to sit, pull out our glasses, and pour us a glass of wine. Chrissy's fiancé, Keith, arrived about 10 minutes later, and we wave him down to come join us. I used to feel like a third wheel, but over the years, it has just become the norm, but I try to give them their space. He has always accepted our bond because she is an only child, and I'm the closest she has to a sibling. As the instructor makes an announcement that we will begin in about five minutes, I lose focus as this brother who appears to be a little taller than me, with glowing brown skin like he bathes in cocoa butter, enters the room. He knew he was fine; I could see it all over his gorgeous face. Chrissy must have noticed my daze because she laughs and invites him to come over by waving him down, letting him know we have an extra seat. She always did embarrassing shit like that, so I kick her under the table, and I start fixing myself up. I didn't have on anything spectacular because we were going to paint; I was wearing some fitted blue jeans with a loose fitted oversized yellow top, my hair shiny and big, showing off my black curls, and some sandals with a little makeup.

I can see from the corner of my eye that he took Chrissy up on her offer as he takes the empty seat to the right of me. In a deep and sexy tone, he introduces himself. "Hello everyone, I am Isaiah King." Damn, I hadn't been next to a man that ever had me speechless; I couldn't do anything but smile, so Chrissy introduces me as her best friend/sister, Jahiri, and Keith her, fiancé (at the time). I can hear Keith whisper in Chrissy's ear, laughing, "tell Jahiri to stop undressing that man with her eyes." I wasn't going to say anything to him that night because he made me nervous. I think he could tell, so once we started, he told me that he is going to need my help with his painting because he is a virgin when it comes to painting. I would usually think that was corny, but I knew he was trying to make me laugh, and it worked. I loosened up also with the help of the wine Chrissy kept pouring in my cup. I had a great time; we exchanged numbers, and we hung out when we could.

Over that next month, I let him know that I was preparing for graduate school, working full time and interning so I wouldn't have much leisure time, and he respected that. I also knew he would be traveling a lot and that he will still be residing in LA for now because he owned a gym out there. He expressed to me how Architecture is his career, but fitness is his passion. He always wanted to combine the two by designing his own gyms, franchising them, and implementing his fitness model. We became close instantly. We talked on the phone daily, and we always hung out when he came into town. I really liked him, but the truth of the matter is that I was attracted to the image that he wanted me to see. He was a good guy, always knowing just the right thing to say; however, he had a case of the wandering eye when a pretty woman walked by. We were never in a committed relationship, so I didn't make a fuss, but I think it was a little disrespectful. At first, it seemed as though he wanted to make our relationship more serious but with school, work, interning all while trying to help Sabrina, I had too much going on to really fit in a guy that I kind of liked so I distant myself from him, and he soon got the point. He would still call, text, and sometimes send nice cards or flowers to let me know that he was thinking of me, but eventually, that stopped. Chrissy told me that she believed he had gotten back with a girlfriend in LA but wasn't sure because the information came from one of her messy co-workers, so she wasn't sure how true it was and I wasn't pressed to find out. At that point in my life, I was focused on obtaining my degree so I could open my business. I hadn't thought about him in years. But when he randomly reached out to me after all this time has gone by, I started to think about all the "what ifs", which made me miss the thought of what could have sparked between us.

While carrying the last box from my room into the living room, I hear a knock at the door. It was Isaiah; he called a week ago to let me know he would be in town and said he wanted to meet. I asked him if his girlfriend would be okay with that; he just laughed, saying that he sensed some jealousy. I let him know that I wasn't jealous, just curious. He had this mindset that he was the guy that everyone wanted, which may be true for some, but at times, he was a little too cocky for my liking. He finally told me that she wasn't for him and broke up with her about seven months ago. He said that he really wanted to see me and catch up if I had time. I knew he was taking a dig at me, but hell, I did not care. I told him I was moving the day he said he would be in town. Surprisingly, he said he would come help. Damn, I can't believe he is at my door. And just like that, I had butterflies like the first day I saw him.

Chapter 4: Too Much Too Fast

"Well, hello, beautiful," I hear him say as he reached over to hug me. Isaiah was very assertive, athletic, business savvy, kind of conceited, but overall, pretty cool to be around. My heart melted. I leaned in to hug him back, he smelled so good and looked even better wearing those basketball shorts and t-shirt. He could make anything look good. We talked for a quick second, but the movers were trying to finish up to head to my new house that Chrissy helped me find for rent because I wasn't ready to buy a home since it's just me.

After getting to the new house and the movers were gone, I offered to order pizza if he wanted to stay. Without hesitation, he took me up on my offer and began to put my bed up for me. We laughed and talked like old times. I asked him if he had kids now. He stopped what he was doing and gave a pause and said yes. I was shocked, he was older than me, but I didn't know he had kids. He laughed, but I didn't see what was funny, so he jumped up and tried to hug me, but I pulled away, asking how old is his child? "Unfortunately, I don't have any kids or any on the way. I just wanted to see your reaction, and from your expression, I think you might still like me. But if you want, we can work on having a child once I finish putting this bed together". I rolled my eyes, letting him know that his comment was not funny to me, so he changed the subject. "You still have the most gorgeous hazel eyes, Jahiri, and your sassiness is still one of my favorite traits about you. You are probably the only girl that I have ever encountered that just doesn't rock to my every move. You are different."

Isaiah then sat me down and told me that he missed me and asked if I missed him. I didn't answer. "I wanted to link up again to see if, at this point in your life, you were ready to make you and I official?" I still didn't say anything. I was in total shock; I mean, he and I hadn't talked seriously in a very long time, so this was just new to me. At this point, he was getting frustrated. "I am not asking to be your man today, but I'm older, and I really have been thinking about you. I just wanted to see if you wanted to try dating again, I mean for real this time?" The doorbell rang, the pizza was here and I was glad. I ran to the door and paid for the pizza; when I went to sit the pizza on the counter, Isaiah had his shoes on and was reaching for his keys. "I don't know what I was thinking coming back into your life trying to start up where we left off. I didn't even ask if you were dating anyone. I am sorry for wasting your time today, but it truly was good seeing you again."

I let that man walk out of my house without uttering a word. I mean, hell, he just came back into my life; what was the rush about. But that entire night, I couldn't sleep, and I could smell his cologne on my bed from him putting it together for me. I questioned myself a lot that night. Why didn't I want to try to be in a relationship with Isaiah? I liked him from what I could remember. He was an okay guy from the short period that we did hang out, but I really didn't know much about him, not to the point I wanted to call him my man.

The next morning, I got dressed, and I just could not get Isaiah out of my head. I wanted to see him, but I didn't know where he was staying, so I put my pride aside and called him. After two rings, he answered. It was a little after six on a Saturday morning, so I know he had to be sleeping. "I apologized for calling so early, but I wanted to know if you had time today if we could meet and talk?" "If brunch will work for you, then I am down to meet up." I was hoping he said breakfast because brunch was a long time to have this on my mind. At 12:15, I see him walk through the door with a nice suit on. He greeted me with a fake hug. "Hello, I don't have much time, about an hour I have a client to meet soon" "that's fine. I just wanted to speak with you about yesterday. First, you hit me with a surprise. It was like you were trying to force me into a relationship right then and there, and to be honest, we hung out a short period, and I don't know you that well. Secondly, I honestly haven't been in a serious relationship after well…after I was truly hurt by someone I loved. After thinking last night, I realized that I really do miss our friendship, and I wouldn't mind having you back in my life to see what happens from there." "I like that idea. I am trying to find out if you really had time to date this time around; you know you were a woman on a mission back then." "Well, I was upfront with you from the beginning, but I am willing to make time for you now. Just be open and honest with me. I hate wasting my time." "I like that. I like that a lot. And I think I can do that. Let's give it a try."

Chapter 5: Reality Hits Home

Seven months have passed since I received my MBA. I was still working as an entry-level art designer because every time I went out for a higher position, I was told I didn't meet the qualifications which I didn't understand. If you asked me, I exceeded them, but there was always someone better suited for the position, so they say. Well, that was until today when I was let go due to budget cuts. That wasn't my dream job, but it was paying my bills and allowing me to live comfortably. I was still interning with the design company on weekends, but that pocket change wasn't going to pay my bills. To make things worse, I still hadn't landed a business loan for my Boutique. I had worked so hard on my business proposal anticipating it being a breeze after school, but little did I know that they make you jump through so many loops still to just deny you the loan. I don't know how many times I applied and was turned down each time for another reason, which really started to frustrate me. I hated to fail at anything, but this battle, I was losing, and each loan officer would give me a different load of bull when I asked why I was denied. After continuous denials for my business loan and career application rejections, it seemed like the world was telling me that I was worthless. Being fired dropped the bottom out of my dignity—a low that I never imagined. I was in a constant battle with myself. Here I am, a two-time college graduate, no job, no income, denied numerous opportunities all while seeing so many people around me progress in life, and it hurts to the core. I couldn't cry, I wouldn't cry, but I needed to.

Back home, I reflected on my goal to save $10,000 from undergraduate school until now, but when I had to take on that high as rent by myself when helping Sabrina, I ended up with about $3,562.18. That apartment was way overpriced and extremely over my budget. Hell, I didn't have enough for all of the products that I would need for my shoe line to even attempt to open a store, and now, I will have to survive off of my savings until I find another job. I have to admit I didn't like being a "brochure maker" for that company; every day, I was going through the motion so routine, which is why I refused to let my intern go. It was fun and exciting even though I didn't get to make much I was still in an environment that inspired me. I enjoyed my intern, but I was helping someone else live out their dream, and mine was just getting further and further away. I knew I could ask my family for help, but that shit would make Eve right, that my dream doesn't create sustainability. My dream is my dream for a reason, so it will create sustainability for me. I just haven't figured it out just yet, but I will. So, I am not going to tell anyone that I got laid off from my job, especially right before the holidays. I have so much on my mind, but it's time for me to head home to Illinois for the holidays. Being surrounded by my family is always an escape from my problems; home was my happy place.

The night before my flight, Eve called. I could detect that she had some tea to spill through the tone of her voice, but I waited patiently and continued the small talk with Eve until she brought whatever it was up in the conversation. After being on the phone for about ten minutes, laughing and joking Eve finally asked…

"Hey Hiri, just wondering, how is Sabrina doing?"

"I'm not sure haven't spoken with her since she moved. I mean, I reached out, but she hasn't responded, and I'm not kissing her ass when I haven't done anything to her. She always does little stupid shit like that. Why, what's up?"

"Well, I saw her a couple of days ago, and she is pregnant!!"

"Oh yea, she did give me that scoop right before she left (laughing). Damn, I thought I told you?"

"Well, you didn't tell me. I didn't know she was pregnant. Did she tell you who the father is?"

"No, she gave me some bull crap of him being someone from back home I didn't know, so I didn't press for more information. Maybe, he was a one-night stand (giggling); you know she can be a wild child. But maybe she will tell me soon. Or at least if she invites me to the baby shower, I will meet him there."

"Jahiri, I don't know how to tell you this because I know you two were like sisters even when you two don't talk for a while, but you need to know. Sometimes people are convenient friends, or you may simply outgrow people. Are you following me?"

"Well, no, but I get the gist of what you are saying. I don't understand why you are saying it."

"At your graduation, I saw Chris. He and Sabrina were talking. When I asked why he was there, she said that he had a frat brother graduating from the school."

"Okay, so what is the big deal?"

"Well, a couple of days ago, I saw them with another guy and girl at the mall, but when I tried to speak to her, she wobbled off so fast, and Chris just held his head down as if he didn't recognize me."

"Wow..."

I was obviously shocked and confused with the information that I just received from my sister, so I quickly changed the topic "Will you be coming to get me from the airport in the morning?" "Whatever, Jahiri, I know you are changing the topic, but no, Ma will, because the boys are out of school, and I don't want to wake them so early they are demons in the morning, so we will meet you all at *Portillo's* for lunch." We talked for another hour with excitement, preparing to spend time with one another. She can be a real jerk, but I love her. We finally ended the call so I could finish packing and prepare to go to the airport in the morning.

"Calling Boarding Zone three," I could hear the flight attendant voice over the loud intercom waking me from my nap. It was time for me to board the plane. I'm usually very excited to go home to be with my family and best friend, but I had so many unanswered questions regarding Sabrina, not to mention losing my job and still no idea what I am going to do next... I was feeling all fucked up. I tried not to think about it, so I put my earphones in and went to sleep.

Chapter 6: Holiday Surprises

"There is my baby" I could hear a loud woman yelling from across the airport, and without looking, I knew it was my mother. My mom was no shy woman; in fact, she was the total opposite. She is a very outgoing woman who voiced her opinions. She is a very caring, nurturing, passionate, hardworking, driven lady who raised her daughters to be independent but to know how to love a man. Although, she had not gone to college, she owned a daycare for over 20 years. She loved children and wanted to be able to provide childcare for working parents in her community. She now has two daycares with the help of my father and sister, who wanted to see her business grow in hopes that it could be a thriving family business. She loved the idea and has been doing well overseeing them both for several years now. She is well respected within our city, and so many people love her.

I turn around; there she is, a beautiful mocha woman wearing a black coat, hat, scarf, sweats, and these hideous red snow boots that she found on clearance a couple of years ago. My mom has lived up north her entire life, so she is always dressed for the weather. As a kid, she always made me wear these horrendous snowsuits that were a struggle to put on and off before and after school, but I must admit, walking in the snow to and from school I was quite warm. "Hey, Ma! I am so happy to see you and those boots!" I reach in and hug my mom for a moment longer than I usually would, but she knew that I needed some extra love, so she held me in her arms as only she could. I missed her. She is the only woman in the world that could make me feel better just by her hug; it's a mother's touch; there is nothing like it. It's like she gives off some of her strength, courage, love, compassion, whatever it is that I need at the moment. It seems like she provides it to me through that pat on the back. I'm what Eve calls a "mama's girl." It was true, my mother and I talked all the time because, with her, I could be so carefree and just be myself. In life, I felt I was always on a mission to prove something, but with my mom, there was nothing to prove; I knew that she loved me no matter what because her love was genuine and purely unconditional. Although I knew my mom would give unsolicited advice on my life, I knew that it was all out of love and that no matter what I did, she would always be there for me. My family was hella annoying, but I loved them all.

We left the airport heading to *Portillo's* for lunch since I ended up having a two-hour delay this morning at the airport; my mouth was watering for that Italian beef. On the ride to our favorite restaurant, my mom cut the radio all the way down, which didn't seem unusual because she always wanted to catch up when we hadn't seen one another in a while. My mom was very blunt, and today was no different.

"I ran into Sabrina's mom yesterday. She seems to be doing better and looking better these days, but what she told me was just heartbreaking. I always knew Sabrina did some things as a child acting out to get attention and even did some spiteful things to you, which made her appear not to be a good friend in my eyes, but I knew she had it hard growing up. I just didn't know she would take it so far, even after all you have done for her. Yeah, I also learned that you had been paying all the bills while you two lived together, how the hell you managed that I don't know, and I don't think you should have done it, but it's done now.

"What, Ma? What did she do? Acting as if what Eve had just told her the night before doesn't have my blood boiling."

"Well, hell to make a long story short, she said Sabrina had become very distant during the pregnancy but came around the past month because she wanted help with her baby shower. She went on to say that she knew that Sabrina was using her to finance the baby shower, but she was her only girl, so she helped. When Ms. Patton asked Sabrina if our family would be coming to the baby shower, she told her no because you haven't talked to her since she moved. She thought you two were just going through something, but she said, at the baby shower, Chris came, and she didn't understand why he would be there. Supposedly, he is the father. He is denying that he is the father, and at the baby shower, he came to tell her to stop putting that lie out in the world. But Sabrina is sticking to the story that he is the father and seems to be happy about it. This is a new low, even for her."

"What do you mean, her child's father?"

"Girl, you heard what I said. That's her baby daddy."

I dazed out for a moment. Growing up, I knew it was hard for Sabrina because her father just got up and left her mom with no explanation, which put her mother in a deep depression. Her mom eventually went to counseling, which provided healing for her, but Sabrina never got to talk to anyone. Well, when her mother remarried and began to have kids with her stepfather, Sabrina started to act out and do some of the craziest things. Sometimes she even did mean things to me, but I forgave her because she would tell me how she was feeling, and I understood that she was hurting. I was a kid, though, so I didn't know how to help her. I just wanted to be there for her, so she didn't feel alone. Breaking my daze, I hear my mom through smacking on that banana she was eating.

"Your nephews are happy to see you, and they have a list of shit they want y'all to do while you are here. You have to stop spoiling them little demon seeds because that good kid act, they throw on you is such a façade."

I look at my mom, and we both bust out to laughing as we continue to the restaurant where Eve and the twins are waiting, which she has let us know for the third time with all of her text. She is so impatient, but sometimes I think the twins know how to work her nerves. Eve is seventeen years older than me, and she waited later in life to have kids because she wanted to accomplish her goals before entering into parenthood. I love how the twins keep her on her toes. She takes on a serious role all the time, but when she had the twins, she became a little softer sometimes. She tried to keep that "I am in charge" demeanor with them, but they let her know from pregnancy that they are in charge, and they say some of the things that even she cannot help but laugh.

"Auntie Hiri, here we are!" I saw Zachariah flagging me down with his coloring book. He is the jokester that keeps me laughing all while I am at home. "Hi Auntie Hiri, did you bring me anything?" I reached down and give my nephews a hug and kissed them on the forehead ignoring Zachariah's question. He didn't take that well because he didn't hug me back; instead, he folded his arms and pouted. Zarie passed me a picture that he made for me. "Here, I made this for you to put up in your house." "Thank you, man; I think I will put this on my refrigerator with the other pictures you made for me." "You're welcome, did you see that car set I sent you that I wanted for Christmas? If you weren't able to get it, it's okay, but I really wanted it, Auntie Hiri." "You two will have to wait until Christmas to find out if I brought you anything." By this time, my mom, Eve, and I are looking back and forth at each other internally laughing at how the boys ganged up on me in such a short period. They associate me visiting to gifts and activities, but I created those monsters.

Eve ordered our food right before we pulled in and it was ready about ten minutes after we sat down. I said grace and took the first bite of my sandwich. It was so good. We sat and talked for a while, then my mom and I left to the grocery store to finish getting all of the things she would need for Christmas dinner. The crowds were out as always during this season, which is why I am glad she didn't need much.

Chapter 7: Toast of Christmas EVE

It was the morning of Christmas Eve, and I hadn't seen or spoken to Sabrina phony ass since I've been home. And to believe in college, she was the one calling me all the time telling me about all the things Chris was doing out here. Her ass failed to mention that he was doing it with her. Chris and I met at a summer fair right before our sophomore year of high school. We went to different schools, but we lived in the same neighborhood. We dated up until my first semester of college. We vowed that we would make things work after high school. He claimed he wanted to go to school with me, but his basketball scholarship was better at the college at home, so he stayed there for school. At first, things were cool, but then, he became very distant, and without me asking, Sabrina would call and tell me the shit he was out there doing. Our families said we might not make it through college, and they wanted us to venture out and explore life, but they never forced a break upon us; they just let it unfold. Well, eventually, it happened, and I was so sad, but it did help me focus more on school and enjoy my college experience. I was able to not focus on a relationship but myself, which really motivated me to change my major, but Eve still thinks it was because of heartbreak. I was hurt by our breakup back then, but I eventually got over it. I dated other people, but nothing serious. I became more fixated on my career goals and life aspirations, not having to take on the stress of other people for the first time. Which was good because college was a task within itself; I no longer had my mother to wake me up, fix me breakfast, and remind me to do my assignments. I quickly learned to be self-sufficient, but I think my parents and Eve really drilled that into me growing up, but being the baby, I was kind of spoiled now that I think about it.

I was finally dressed; I walked downstairs wearing my decorated Christmas hat that my nephew Zaire made for me. His brother Zachariah made his moms because he claimed that I wouldn't rock it right; he too had no sense of fashion like his mother. My mom was in the kitchen cooking for tomorrow. She always made a big meal, but she cooked extremely slow so she had to start the day before and sometimes we still would have dinner late. As usual, I could hear Eve before I saw her. She was singing Christmas carols, and my dad was yelling, telling her to shut up. She came into the kitchen and asked if I was ready to go to the mall with her to do some last-minute shopping. Before I could answer, my dad yelled out, "and take these worrisome ass boys with you." He loved those twins, but they knew how to work his nerves, especially when he wanted to watch the game or take a nap.

At the mall, Eve was acting really strange; it was something about her that just wasn't right. I mean for once, she was being overly nice. For a minute, I thought it was about the Sabrina and Chris situation, but she has always shown tough love so for this situation, I didn't expect anything different from her. I knew that couldn't be it. I would catch her reading a text followed by a smile as if she just won a million dollars. She received a phone call and walked off as if she didn't want me to hear her conversation. I figured it was her husband, Thomas, sending her nasty messages, so I didn't press the issue. But when I took the boys to ride the merry go round, she quickly freshened up her lipstick and was fixing her curls. She gave me some extra money to let the boys ride again, which, normally, she wouldn't even stop to let them ride it. "Hey Jahiri, I am going to a toy store to get another gift for the twins, and I don't want them to see it, so stay with them and keep them occupied" "Okay, I will. Get me that purse that you were just looking at in the last store and you have a deal." "Here, I am not getting you a $500 purse just for you to watch your nephews." "Well, don't take too long; you know they get antsy very quickly and there is not much that I can do to keep them entertained in the mall." "I will be right back, stop whining; you sound like them. Here is some money just in case they say they are hungry." I wanted to roll my eyes, but I feared her like I did my parents, so I just grabbed

the money turning back at the boys, who were smiling with enthusi-
asm. I looked back, and I saw Eve being approached by a pretty good-
looking older man; well, he appeared to be in his forties as she was.
My sister had no style, but she was drop-dead gorgeous. She was
about 5'7", rocked a pixie cut, she worked out all the time, so her
body was on point with a beautiful brown skin and light brown eyes.
I figured the guy was trying to hit on her, but the way she hugged him
was as if they knew each other. She was giggling hard then they
turned the corner, and I couldn't see l what they did next.

About forty-five minutes later, Eve met us at the food court because the boys were over the Farris Wheel and complained that they
were starving because they hadn't eaten all day. I knew that to be a lie
because I watched them demolish pancakes, eggs, bacon, hash brown,
and fruit about two hours ago. If I hadn't seen them eat, their speech
would have made me believe they hadn't eaten in weeks. Before Eve
could even sit down, Zachariah bust out, "mom, where have you been
because you were gone for a long time, and Auntie Hiri said she was
ready to go." I wanted to pop him in the mouth; he is such a snitch.
"Well, tell her how you had a full-blown tantrum because they didn't
have the toy you wanted in your happy meal." "I thought you weren't
going to tell her?" "Well, you ran your mouth, so I figured it was fair."
"Please stop arguing with a seven-year-old. And Zach, I was minding
my business. Stay in a child's place." She popped him on his hand,
and the two gave each other some kind of stare off. He was so much
like Eve with that smart mouth. To keep him from getting in too much
trouble, I asked her if she found the gifts she was looking for. She said
yes, but I didn't see her with any new bags. "I already put them in the
car. Are you all ready to go?" "Yes, I am, mommy." "Me too,
mommy." We were finally preparing to leave the mall, and I was so
happy because the twins were a handful. As we were putting the bags
in the trunk, I didn't see any bags from a toy store; however, there was
a small bag from *Zales* tucked over in the corner. I didn't ask about it
because I feared being popped in the mouth.

Later that night, we all went over to Eve's house for her annual
"Toast of Christmas Eve" I wasn't sure if she called it that because it
was actually Christmas Eve or if she was just vain and it had something to do with her name. All I do know is that it was always fun. My
sister always went out the way for her parties with the décor, food,
drinks, and even the gift giveaways. This year was no different. I was

having a good time laughing and mingling with family and friends when my mom pulled me to the side, "has Eve, said anything to you about her and her Thomas?" Before I could answer, she continued on to say, "the twins asked if they could still come over tomorrow for Christmas as usual, and so I asked them why wouldn't they be able to? The twins basically told me that their father lived with Ms. Bridgett (their father's ex-girlfriend who he supposedly broke up with months before he met my sister), and she was giving them a little sister for Christmas." "Damn" was the first thing that came out of my mouth, forgetting that I was talking to my mom. Sipping on her wine, she replied, "right," nodding her head in agreement as she walked off.

Chapter 8: A Strange Christmas

The next morning, all I could hear was _Mommy Kissing Santa Clause_ by _Michael Jackson_ coming from the kitchen. As I was walking towards the kitchen, I, unfortunately, heard my dad tell my mom, "I better not find out you were kissing no damn Santa because I didn't have my Santa suit on last night." Disgusted, I tried to walk back towards my room, but I had been spotted, and they laughed demanding that I come back to the kitchen. My parents, after all these years, were still sexual with one another, and sometimes it was just something I did not care to see. Anyone who knew them could tell that their relationship was built off a strong friendship because they always acted like best friends. They did everything together, and it wasn't that they didn't have other friends because they did it was just that they just enjoyed doing things with one another. They argued and had disagreements, and my mom had a mouth that was like a sharp knife when she was upset, but they always fought harder to get through hard times together.

My mom was still cooking dinner for tonight, which was normal, no matter how early she started. I was so glad I brought a plate from Eve's party last night because I knew I wouldn't be getting breakfast, and for some reason, when I come home, I don't like to buy food or cook because I loved eating my mom's cooking. I sat there eating my leftover rotel and wings for breakfast while my dad began to ask when I was going to get married and have him a granddaughter. He annoyed me with that question. "When I hit the lotto, have three successful businesses, a personal assistant, and Nanny, Dad." "Well damn, I guess you are not having kids any time soon." Shrugging my shoulders eating on another chip thinking I had a plan that I haven't began to accomplish, so I wasn't ready for marriage or kids; that was actually the furthest thing from my mind at this point in my life. That always frustrated my parents. They emphasized to me that I need to learn how to live through the process because life doesn't go as planned and things will happen that you will never be prepared for. I never really understood what they meant by living through the process; I mean, what else would I be doing. They wanted me to know that I wasn't getting any younger and to take advantage of life while I have the opportunity. They didn't go to college, but they were successful business owners. In one breath, it's go to school, get your education and use it to better yourself all while taking advantage of learning opportunities outside of the classroom to know as much as possible. But in another breath, slow down and have a family. How those two make sense, I don't understand. Truth be told, I think I was an accident child; I mean, why else wait seventeen years later. My mom tells me all the time how she was working so hard to get her daycare up and running when she got pregnant with me, so having another child was not on their radar. I get my drive to be successful from them, and I wanted them to see that without coming off disrespectful, but instead of a debate, I changed the subject.

Christmas was different; I would usually stay over at Eve's house to watch my nephew open gifts, but last night, she basically told me to go home. I didn't put up a fight only because I know she and her husband were going through some things. She is very secretive, and we all know not to ask her anything about her business or she would give an explosive response, depending on how angry it made her she would not talk to us for months. She loved to be in everyone else business; however, when it's done to her, it's considered to be disrespectful and out of line. I learned as a kid to just let her be; it made life easier.

Eve arrived around noon, and she seemed super happy as she always does during the holidays, but she didn't have the twins. "Where are the boys?" "Oh, they're with their dad at his parents' house. He will bring them by later today. We all knew that was some bullshit because even before the kids were born, she fought to have Christmas with our parents, and with her attitude, we know she won because they had been there for the past six years even Thomas's parents would come over sometimes. No one bothered to get her to tell the truth because we all knew she would have a great come back, and it wasn't worth the energy. Eve and I begin to talk when the doorbell rang. It was very early for guests, even for our family, who makes up their own arrival time. My dad called me to the front door, and I hadn't made plans for anyone to stop by, so I anxiously walked to the front door and, to my surprise, it was him standing there, and I was lost for words.

Chapter 9: Unexpected Guest

I hesitated as I approached the door; I mean, I was in shock that he was standing so close to me. I hadn't seen him in person since the morning we said our goodbyes the morning my parents were preparing to take me to Atlanta for school freshman year. It's like he made himself disappear every time that I came home to visit, and now that all this has happened, he is standing in my front door. My dad walks away, and I immediately feel a burst of different emotions erupt anger, rage, hurt, and confusion. I mean, it's like emotions I didn't know that I had just resurfaced. Chris, standing at my door looking dumbfounded, opens his mouth and says, "Jahiri Strong, it's been a long time, and you still look amazing." I hope he didn't think I was going to react to that. "Hey, well, I know I am the last person you expected to see this morning, but I have had a lot on my mind, and I've wanted to reach out to you for years, but I didn't know how to. Look, I'm sorry for how I ended things with you back in the day. I was young, immature, and really feeling myself on campus as a popular athlete. It was messed up how I just started ignoring you and entertaining other girls, but again, I was young. If I could do it all over again, I would do it differently; I promise. It was messed up for sure that I broke up with you in a text because I couldn't bear to hear the pain in your voice. That's all me, and I apologize. Well, with all that I know you have been hearing, I wanted to come over and personally tell you sorry for that which I wish I had the courage to do years ago but didn't. But now I needed you to hear from me face to face that I have too much respect and love for you as a person to ever stoop so low to mess with your best friend" He looks me dead in the eyes and grabs my arms; the arms that are folded. "I would never ever do that, Jahiri, and I needed you to hear this from me. I would never do that to you." My eyes are now filled with tears because I never in a million years thought I would ever hear an apology come from his mouth. I wanted to be strong, but a tear fell from my eye.

"Look, I know it may be hard for you to believe me, but I am telling you the truth. Sabrina came up here a month before your graduation, and I was drunk at my friend moving party when she popped up. I don't even know who invited her, but she was really upset with you and your new life. She said you changed which is to be expected; we aren't kids anymore, but I really wasn't trying to hear her talk bad about you, I mean I know she was the one telling you all the foul shit I was doing out here back in the day, so she was not on my friend list. But that's beside the point. She came on to me sexually a few times, and I knew she had to be drunk, so I tried to get her a car home, but she was adamant about staying at the party, so I left her alone and she went around the party dancing with a few guys and girls that night. I was a little too drunk to be driving, so my boy let me crash on his bed for an hour, but about thirty minutes into me laying in the bed, Sabrina wakes me up naked, saying how she wanted me. Now, I know Sabrina to be a wild child, but I never anticipated her doing anything like that. I pushed her off me and went out of the room. Well, my fiancée" came to the party looking for me because I wasn't responding, and as I was leaving the room, there she is, looking at me and Sabrina standing behind me naked. She didn't believe me, and I don't blame her, but I know I didn't touch Sabrina, and she is refusing to tell the truth. I may have lost the love of my life all because of some bullshit. Yea, you are probably thinking this is a load of shit too or karma for how I treated you, but I really needed to come over here and tell you the truth."

The house door swung open really fast, followed by Eve yelling, "what the hell is he doing here? Jahiri, are you alright?" "I am fine. Go back in the house." Eve rolled her eyes at me and gave Chris the longest vicious stare down before she finally decided to close the door. That again shows how she likes to be nosy in my business but is walking around here living a damn lie. Chris, now with a smirk on his face, "your sister has never liked me" defensively, "you've given her a few reasons not to."

"Jahiri, I know this is all crazy, and I wish this wasn't the reality right now, but it is. I just want you to know that again, I am sorry for how we ended in college, and when Sabrina has the baby, I will be getting a DNA test to prove that the baby is not mine."

"That doesn't mean you didn't have sex with her."

"My fiancée says the same thing. But the thing is after I graduated a few years ago I changed. I am no longer that goofy teen you use to date. I am a man with aspirations to be a husband and have a family. I love my fiancé, and I would never do anything to lose her; she means the world to me. Seeing her hurt really made me think of how I made you feel back then, and those feelings resurfaced. Being the man that I am today; I am apologizing for how I treated you back then and even putting myself in a situation for Sabrina to begin this lie."

I did not want to believe him, but the sincerity in his voice was convincing, and the fact that he never once denied his cheating when I brought it to his attention back then made it hard not to believe him. Moreover, he got caught cheating, so he had to admit it. He turned around the next day and broke up with me in a text. So why lie to me now when he has no ties to me at this point. He seemed to be in love with whoever this woman is, and she really made an impact on him for him to come over and apologize to me after all these years, so I was really believing him or at least wanted to.

"Thank you, Chris, for coming over to apologize to me. I have to admit, I never wanted an apology from you, but I think parts of me needed it. I hope that your fiancé finds it in her heart to forgive you in whatever scenario is the truth."

"I don't know how you do, but you always find it in your heart to be nice even when you are hurting. That's a strength that I wish I had. But thank you for hearing me out, and yeah, I hope she does too, but unlike you, she isn't so forgiving. Don't get me wrong she knows how to hold a grudge the way you do, but she isn't so forgiving."

"Yeah, well, unlike me, she hasn't had enough time to process things, so give her that. And next time, don't put yourself in that position. Call her and tell her to come pick you up, you fucking drunk."

"You're right, you're right."

"Well, I have to get back to helping my mom. Again, I hope everything works out for you."

"Continue to take care of yourself. Thank you for hearing me out, and again, I truly apologize. I want you to find happiness with someone again. Oh, and I will be on the lookout for your shoe store. I know it's going to be lit."

I smile as I walk towards the door thinking, how did he know about my shoe store and what made him think I hadn't found happiness with anyone since him. What was Sabrina telling him? I don't know, but that made me feel a little bit more like a failure. "Bye, Chris." I closed the door as he walked off. I hurried to the downstairs bathroom, but before I could get there, the tears eased their way down my cheek. I was crying because he was right; I hadn't been able to give anyone a real chance at love because I didn't want to feel that kind of hurt again. Then for him to think that after all these years, he has that type of power over my emotions made it worse. I cried and released all of the resentment, hurt and anger that I have been blindly carrying on my shoulders for far too long. I hear a heavy knock at the door it was my father. He didn't say a word; I just knew it was him. I reached to open the door as I was sitting on the floor looking up at this tall man with his grey and white beard. He walked in and sat on the floor beside me, still not uttering a word. He put me in his arms and let me cry for a bit longer. He was my protector; still to this day, and this moment was no different. He let me know by his action that I was going to be okay. My mom came looking for my dad and found us sitting on the restroom floor. She didn't ask. It's as if she already knew. She allowed my dad to be there for me at that moment. "Hey, where is everyone?" Eve was approaching the restroom. "Girl, here I am. Come help me fix the rest of these pies." "Where are daddy and Jahiri?" "They are catching up; he hasn't gotten the opportunity to bond with her since she has been home, so let them be and come and help me like I asked you." "Okay, Ma, I was just asking." I could hear their voice fade away.

"Dad, I really hope she doesn't let her help cook anything." We both started laughing as he reaches down, helping me to get up off the floor. "I hope she doesn't either, Jahiri." My dad is a man of few words, but when it comes to emotions, you gather his love through his actions. I loved and admired my father. He is stern in his ways, but I know he will always be there for me without hesitation. We walked in the living room, and I sat to watch the parades with him on tv. We talked and caught up on all the sports and current events. My father was a selftaught man, but you would think he went to the finest university if you had a conversation with him. That is until the twins come around to disturb his peace. It's like they are the only ones who can make him curse and test his patience. I find it quite amusing watching him now versus when I was growing up.

Later that evening, our family and friends arrived, and the fun activities began. Kids were playing with their new toys, my aunts in the kitchen drinking their wine bragging on what their husbands got them for Christmas and the fella's playing cards or watching the game. We eventually all got together as a whole because my mom always forced us to play family games, and the kids put on a talent show. You could tell the parents were in competition because some of the costumes and props were sometimes over the top; needless to say, still very entertaining. You could tell even though everyone complained that they actually enjoyed the Christmas "gameathon". The twins made it just in time, and from the smiles on their faces, we could tell they were happy to be there too. My day started off rocky and emotional but ended on a high note.

Chapter 10: Email Reply

It was two days after Christmas, and I was awakened by vibrations coming from my nightstand. It was six in the morning, and my mom was calling to make sure that I had made it home safely. She still doesn't know that I don't have my full-time job, which is why she is calling so early; I would normally be up by now. When I answered, I just told her I took the day off. This made her ask why I didn't stay longer but pretended as if I had another call to hurry her off the phone. I got up and got dressed for the gym to complete a small workout before I start my day. Once I was finished, I got dressed and realized that I really have nothing to do. I checked my email to see if I had gotten any interview emails. I hadn't, but it was holidays so I figured that I wouldn't. I then saw an email from Ms. Kelly; she is the owner of the design company I intern at part-time. She sent out an email blast asking if anyone wanted to pick up extra hours during this week. They don't pay interns very well, but I could use any extra cash right now, and I have nothing else to do, so I sent her a response, letting her know of my availability. Shockingly, she responded right back and asked if I could start tomorrow morning. I let her know that I would be there.

Later that afternoon, I received a call from Isaiah. "Hello Beautiful, how was work today?" He didn't know I had been laid off either, so I just told him exactly what I told my mom. "Wow, you actually took an extra day off. Well, how was your trip?" I tried to call him a few times back home, and sometimes he did answer, but sometimes he would send me to voicemail, followed by a text letting me know he would call me later. I didn't mind. I figured he was with family, and I was really trying to enjoy time with mine. "My trip was good. I got to spend time with my family and those nephews of mine worked every nerve that I have." "They are so cool; I hope to have a son like them one day." "They are terrible little monsters. Anyways, how was the holiday for you? I tried to call you a few times, but you seemed to be busy." "Yea, I went out of town with my oldest brother and his wife to visit her family; just to get out of town for a minute besides for work." "Oh, wow, I didn't know you were going out of town, you never mentioned it. But cool, I guess. I hope you had a good time." "Yeah, it was a good time. But anyways my birthday is coming up, and I would love for you to come out here and spend it with me. Do you think you will be able to?" "Umm…I am not sure. With work and all… Why didn't you ask earlier?" "I don't know. I just figured you wouldn't be able to; since it's so close to coming back from your holiday break, but I really want to see you." "Well, I don't think I will be able to make it since it is such short notice, but I will see what I can do." "That's all that I ask, but I will be buying you a ticket just in case you are able to." "Okay, well, I will let you know." "Alright, well I am about to head to the gym, I'll call you tomorrow." "Bye."

I was learning that Isaiah was very spontaneous and always wanted things instantly. For me, sometimes it was too much, like when he talked about having kids. I think if I told him that I wanted a child now, he would be happy and down for it. I sometimes think he and I are on two different pages in life, but I continue to show him signs that I am not going to be his wife anytime soon. I just became his girlfriend. Sometimes I think that was a mistake because it really doesn't feel like one being that he is never around or available when I need him or just want to talk. But when he wants something, there is always a sense of urgency. There are times I just wanted to pick up the phone and call it quits with him, but then he does the most charming things like sending flowers or a card expressing how he feels about me making me question myself if I am just looking for a way out of this relationship. The day Chris came to apologize, I had time to reflect, and I thought maybe I treated Isaiah kind of cold because I really wasn't ready to be in a relationship, but when I called him to talk about it, he declined my call twice sending me to voicemail both times. I started to realize that yea, I may have been holding on to some past hurt, but Isaiah wasn't the charming guy that I thought he was back when we first met. But I don't know; maybe I am tripping. I'll think about going to visit him. It's not like I have anything to do, and I will be able to speak with him face to face; body language really tells a lot about how a person really feels.

As I walked into Ms. Kelly's design studio the next morning, it looked different. I guess because I usually only work on weekends when it is full of interns and staff. It was seven in the morning, and she was the only one in the office. "Hello there, I am Vivian Kelly. I haven't had the pleasure of meeting you in person, but I have heard a lot about you. It's nice to finally put a face to your name." "Good morning Ms. Kelly." I was stunned that she claimed to have heard of me. I never had the opportunity to meet her in all of the years that I have worked here. Maybe she was just saying that to make me feel special. "Well, I am glad that you responded to my email. I am usually closed until two weeks after new the year to allow my staff a mental break from the previous year, but for some reason, I forgot about a deadline that I have, and I need all the help I can get. Well, you are the only person who replied, so I will be putting you to work if you are ready?" "Oh, yes, ma'am, I' ready to do whatever you need." Assuming that she needs a secretary since I was familiar with that kind of work. "Great, well, I am launching a new pillow design, and I am having a hard time coming up with a new creative design concept. That's where you come in. I would like you to be the lead designer and come up with the pitch to give to my investors. Don't worry; I know you are cable to; your portfolio, which you submitted when you applied to be an intern is phenomenal, so I know you will come up with something great." So, she really does know who I was. "Well, I only have experience designing shoes, and I've only designed a few tops here and there." "You're a creative designer, so I am confident this will be a breeze for you." "And I have never pitched anything to investors." "I'll help guide you through the entire process, so don't worry, you will not be in this alone. Besides, this is my name and company on the line, so it's a reflection of me. I will not let you fail or look bad." Hesitating and a little uneasy wishing I hadn't responded to the email, I agreed. "I am aware that you only intern on weekends, but this will take some time, so that's what I will have you working on this week, and you can finish up once we open back up on the weekends. I don't want you to use your entire break here." Well, I was just recently laid off, so I honestly don't have anything else to do, but I will need a pay increase." "Of course, in fact, come into my office and let's discuss this a little more."

I walked out of the office thinking, "she is a real boss". She didn't have any open salaried positions at the moment, but she removed me as an intern to interim entry-level designer offering me sixteen an hour with a one-time bonus of two thousand dollars after I complete the presentation to the investors. The only thing is I will only get twenty-five hours a week, but it's better than nothing. I will also be able to enroll in health insurance during annual enrollment on January 1st, which is normally for full-time employees, but she made an exception for me. It wasn't the most, but it put me in a better position than I was in prior to coming to her office this morning. As I sat down at the empty desk outside of her office, I took a moment for a praise break. I was so happy on the inside, I just gained a job (kind of) that I hadn't applied for, and to be honest, I think she just created.

As I sat waiting for her to bring me the books and information that I would need to complete this project, my mom called. I wanted to answer and tell her the good news, but I remembered that she didn't even know that I had been jobless. "Well, here you go, Ms. Strong." She gave me a quick training, but most of the things she showed me were just refreshers of things I had learned in undergraduate school just now I would be applying it to design pillows. It was actually easier than I thought. It felt good to be doing something that I loved, which is having an idea and making it tangible. I enjoyed talking with Ms. Kelly.
She was a really cool woman to be the boss.

"You remind me so much of myself when I was young, Ms. Strong. You are passionate about design; I can tell it comes naturally to you."

"Really, well, I am not that young, and I haven't done anything useful with my designs. They are just pictures of creations that seem like they will never be developed." She laughed, "well, if you don't mind me asking how old are you?" "I'll be 27 in April."

"Well, don't beat yourself up, and if it makes you feel any better, I didn't open my first business until I was 32. It's hard, but you have to stick to it if it's really what you want to do." "What made you keep going?"

"Well, my grandparents raised me, and when they saw how hard it was to get my business started asking more so begging for loans, they sold their house and invested in me. I couldn't fail on them. I was able
to pay them back and buy them a new house."

"I know they are proud of you."

"They were. So don't get discouraged. You may find this hard to believe, but I actually started off making wedding gowns and prom dresses. They did well but nothing compared to my furniture line." "Those are two totally opposite types of design, what made you change your approach. "Well, one day, my Sorror called me up in a panic, asking if I could do custom design in the master bedroom of a house she was trying to sell. I knew she was stressed being that it was her first time selling a house, so I decided to give it a try. Well, I ended up loving it, and when she sold the house, the buyers purchased my bedroom set. I then created a bedding line using the little profit that I had from my gown store. It took about a year and a half before it started to boom, but now I have four locations in different states, so again, I say be patient and allow your dream to lead you to your calling. Trust the process and be sure to live through it."

"My parents say that all the time and I really don't get it, what do you all mean when you say that?" Laughing, "Well, I mean enjoy life, take breaks, hang with friends, have a family just enjoy life, you only get one and time you will never get back. If I could change one thing, I would get married, have a kid and enjoy all of my hard work." After all of these years, I never understood what my parents meant. It took me asking a stranger to explain it to me, and I get it now. After lunch, I went back into the office and began to work more on my assignment. I don't know why, but I walked to Ms. Kelly's office and asked her if I could talk. She waved her hand for me to come in and have a seat. I let her know that I was invited on a trip this weekend and asked if I could take Friday off. Without hesitation, she replied, "Of course you may."   On my ride home, I called Isaiah, and when he answered, I said, "Hey handsome!" He laughed, "that's new; you must have had a good day at work." Yes, I actually had a great day at work, so I will be able to come celebrate your birthday with you." "Great, I already sent your ticket information to your email. I am glad you will be able to come. I don't know what happened today at work, but I hope you remain this cheerful." "Well, we shall see. I will call you later." "Okay, bye, Jahiri." For some reason, I was so happy; I didn't know why but I didn't question it. I enjoyed the moment. I knew for sure that I didn't want a future with him so I didn't want to waste his time any longer so I will let him know face to face that he and I are not for one another.

I worked with Ms. Kelly the remaining time before my trip, and each day was like a new adventure for me, and I enjoyed getting up for work in the morning. That Thursday before my trip, Ms. Kelly told me to take a half-day with pay because I had been putting in so many extra hours that my work is already above schedule. "God, have fun. We can pick back up when you return." I took her up on that offer, and by that Friday afternoon, I was with the guy that had no idea that I was planning to break up with him.

Chapter 11: Sneaky, Sneaky

Isaiah's house was always well put together like something out of a magazine; like it was decorated by a woman. I am on a time difference, so I woke up earlier than he did this morning. He has a gym downstairs of his apartment, so I went to work out. This place is beautiful, but the cost of living out here is just ridiculous. I walk in the gym, and there is no one in sight; just how I like it. I get on the treadmill and run for thirty minutes. It's still dark out, so I pick up a few weights and do some toning exercises. I started working out when I was about twelve. Eve would take me with her on weekends back when she was still in medical school, and I have been doing it ever since. When I finish up my workout, I sit on the floor back pressed against the cold wall; that felt so good I was tired and sweaty. I started to think about how I was going to tell this man that I wanted to just be friends during his birthday weekend. That's fucked up. Maybe I should just wait until I go back home and call him. The door to the gym swings open, interrupting my thoughts, and it was a middle-aged woman with an all red workout suit on walking through the door. From the look on her face, she wasn't expecting anyone to be in the gym, but she gave me a smile, waving good morning. I greeted her back, gathering my towel, phone, and water bottle heading back to Isaiah's apartment. He was still sleeping, so I got my things and went into the guest bathroom to take a shower. When I was getting out, I heard music playing, so I guess he is up now. I got dressed and went into the living room. He was in the kitchen, making a smoothie and offered me one. He tried to give me a kiss, but I kind of hit him with a fake stretch as he was leaning in too.

Isaiah went to take a shower. His phone started to ring. I didn't care to see who was calling, but then whoever it was called again and again. So, I peeped over just to take a quick glance, and the number was not saved. Ten minutes later the number tried to facetime him, and I wanted to answer it but he walked in. I let him know someone had been calling him back-to-back and he may want to make sure everything is okay. He looked at the number. "Oh. It's nothing these scam numbers keep calling my phone." *He is a fucking liar*, I thought to myself. We get dressed to head to his birthday celebration, which included a couple of his friends and some of his family that I really didn't know. As we arrive at the lounge that he has apparently rented out for his birthday, everyone is dressed like they are going to a huge event. I didn't look bad, but I do feel like he had this party planned for a while, which makes me wonder if I was initially not invited. Something is just off about this entire situation. We walk in, and everyone yells, "Happy Birthday!" I step off to the side to fix my heel, and when I look back around, Isaiah vanished, leaving me to feel really awkward. He was making me feel more and more like I was making the right decision. I walk over to the bar and order a drink. "Hey, Miss Lady, I haven't seen you before." "You haven't. Hi, how are you?" "Well, it's nice to meet you with your sexy self." I smile as I walk off from the creepy older gentleman trying to spit game on me. "Well, I see you around Miss Jahiri." Why did I tell him my name?

I am no stranger to doing things on my own, so when the DJ starts playing all of the oldies, I get on the dance floor and dance by myself. Some young lady comes over to me while I am dancing. "Hey, now you know how to party. I'm Neicy, I came here with my friend, but she ditched me to hang with some of her other friends." "That's messed up. I'm Jahiri. I came with the birthday boy, and he ditched me." We both laugh, continuing to dance until that creepy old man tried to slip up behind me. If I had hit him, everyone would have thought I was wrong. "He tried to talk to me when I was sitting at the table." "He approached me at the bar." Neicy continued to talk, but I began to look around the room to see if I saw Isaiah, but he was nowhere to be found. "Hey, I don't mean to cut you off, but I am going to the restroom. I will be back shortly." "Okay, girl, I'll be here or back out on the dance floor if your uncle is gone, haha." "Haha"

As I was walking to the restroom, I notice Isaiah in the corner with an older woman who appears to be crying. I don't know who she was, maybe an aunt or something, so I continue on to the restroom. I go in the stale to use the restroom when two other women enter in the restroom behind me having a conversation. "Jackie, fix yourself up and stop crying. Isaiah loves you; he is just hurt that you had an abortion behind his back. He still loves you; he is just hurting." "But he says he is really going to try and move on this time. I really want us to work on our relationship so that we can move forward with getting married. I am forty-three. I never imagined falling in love with a younger man; I didn't see myself a mother at forty, so I got scared, but if I could go back, I would have his child. I am even willing to have one now. I just want him to forgive me." "He will; just give him time. He was just with you and your family for Christmas. He wants to work on things with you; he is just afraid to admit it." I walk out of the stale towards the sink to wash my hands. "I am so sorry you had to hear all of that." "It's okay, we have all been in love before. I hope he finds it in his heart to forgive you. I'm sure he will." "Thank you." I dry my hands as the two women in the restroom continue talking. I couldn't believe what I just heard, and I couldn't believe that I tried to comfort her, but I could hear the pain in her voice.

Isaiah pops up out of nowhere. "Hey, I am sorry about that I didn't mean to vanish on you like that. I had an unexpected and uninvited guess that I needed to address." "Oh, really, who?" "It doesn't matter he is gone now." I only asked to see if he would be transparent with me, but he couldn't even do that. "Hey, I just got called back to work and I need to get my thing so I can catch this flight in a few hours. May I get the key to your apartment?" "Really, you are just going to get up and leave like that? I haven't even introduced you to anyone. I really want you to stay, Jahiri, can you please stay for me." "I really have to go" "Well, here are the keys, I will be down there next weekend maybe you will have time for me then." "No, I'll probably be out of town with my sister and her husband." "What is that supposed to mean?" "You'll figure it out." He is now standing there looking dumbfounded, and I couldn't take it, so I snatch the key out of his hand when his brother called his name. I headed for the door. When Neicy called my name, I didn't have time for her, but I didn't want to be rude, so I stopped. "Are you leaving?" "Yes, something came up. It was nice meeting you." "Likewise, I'll try to have as much fun as possible; you know, with your uncle around here lurking." "Good luck with that. Haha"

When I arrived at Isaiah's house, I grabbed my things as quickly as possible. I placed his gift along with a note that said…

Isaiah,

I hope you and Vivian can work things out since that's where you spent your holiday. Happy Birthday! Thanks for the trip! P.S. Please don't call me trying to explain. ☺

-J. Strong

Chapter 12: Emotional Wounds Resurfaced

Isaiah made breaking up with him a breeze. I am glad that I hadn't invested too much time and energy with him. He called one too many times for my likings after I left that note so I changed my number. He tried to relay message through Chrissy once, but she put a dead to that quickly. I was home, and back to my reality, my bills were piling up, and money was decreasing just looking at them. I was frustrated, and I didn't have the passion to design any of my own material. In fact, since I have lost my job, I hadn't touched my sketchbook nor attempted any designs. It wasn't going to get me anywhere. I was over the rejection, so I sat there on my computer, filling out several applications for a new job. I used to think running away and not dealing with heavy situations was my strength, but in actuality, it was my weakness that became a defense mechanism to protect me from getting hurt, but the truth is; I still ended up feeling like shit. I needed a bigger salary fast because my health insurance was eating up the little money that I was making working for Ms. Kelly, but I needed it. You just never know what could happen, or at least that is what my father has always said. I already have plans to pay up some of my past due bills once I get that lump sum payment after I finish this project, and she may let me go afterwards, so I need to land a job quickly.

Friday morning, when I got to work, Ms. Kelly called me into her office. I hadn't told her that I was looking for a new job, but I would give her a heads up if I landed anything. I was just about halfway finished with her project, and she had been giving me great feedback. I was going to have it done a few weeks before her projected due date, which made her ecstatic, something about that looking good to her investors. She told me a few weeks ago that she would give me a full day to shadow her so that I could learn how she manages the business side of the company; well today was that day. I loved learning; especially when it was something that I was passionate about. I was getting free knowledge that didn't compare to the tuition that cost a fortune for, and I am not even using my degree.

"So today I will be taking you with me to see the distribution center where all of the items are made. We won't be there too long, but I thought you might want to see how your design will be made in mass production." "Oh, yes, I have never had that experience before. "On the inside I am jumping up and down like a little kid. The thought of something that I will be designing could possibly be sold in stores for people to purchase, that's a big deal to me. We arrive at this large factory where I was able to walk around and look at how things are done. I was fascinated. Next on the agenda was a business lunch with some of her staff. Everyone seemed to like working for Ms. Kelly, and I could see why she really treated people like people and not just her employee. She spoke to everyone and would jump in and help whenever someone needed or struggled. She meant what she said about this being a reflection of her, so she was always willing to put in extra work. After the business lunch, she had to make a few conference calls that were long and draining. I think I nodded a few times, but I think she was to indulge in the meeting to notice. Running a big business is no joke, and I was starting to think just maybe I wasn't ready for that type of responsibility. I wonder if she is trying to give me some type of subliminal message. If so, it is working.

I went home for the day, and yes, I learned a lot, but I was drained, not to mention she was still working when I left. How could you have a social life doing that much work? Maybe she doesn't have a true work-life balance; she did say she chose work over having a family. That is kind of sad; I think she would have been a great mother.

The next morning, I woke up feeling super sick. I think it was from trying all those weird dishes at the lunch meeting. I felt like I had a horrible, so I slept my Saturday away. Chrissy called that night upset because this was the one weekend she was in town, but she gave me a pass because I wasn't feeling well, and we made plans to link up before she leaves again for work. I would have thought she would be done with work by now.

Chrissy arrived earlier than planned as usual. This time, using the spare key that I gave her in case of an emergency. She never respects my boundaries but claims that she will change once I get a real man in my life. "Bitch, why aren't you cooking?" "I thought we decided to go out to eat?" "We did; you are right. This fucking pregnancy brain has me tripping. I am going to eat the rest of the chips you have right here if you don't mind; I am starving." "Well, you're eating them now, so I guess I don't mind." "Girl, Isaiah quit working for my company, but before he left, he tried to speak to me. I walked off on his ass. I think he called me a bitch under his breath too, but I let it slide because I was still on the clock." "What would you have done, hit him with your belly?" "Bitch, yes, fucked him up, hahaha. You ready to go? And can you drive? I really don't have the energy to." "Yeah, sure, come on."

On the way home, we stopped every five minutes so Chrissy could piss. This last time, I had to get over three lanes to take the exit so we could stop at Walgreens. Here she comes now with a bag full of junk food, I bet. "What did you just buy?"

"Two bags of chips, honey bun, twix, and some water to wash all the sugar away." We both laugh.

"Hey, Jahiri, just sit here for a few minutes. I might need to go to the restroom again."

"Okay."

"Hey so what's been going on with work, do you have any new leads on your business loan? Please tell me you have told your parents about your job situation."

"No, I haven't told them, and you better not have said anything to them either, especially Eve."

"I haven't, but I think I should. I noticed that past due light bill on the table when I walked in."

"Yeah, well, don't judge me. Not everyone got their dream job after college. So please don't start that lecturing me today I really don't have the energy."

"Well, you did get offered an Intern at the place you are at now, maybe if you had taken it, you would be in a higher position by now, but you wanted to play it safe doing something you didn't even like; look at you now."

I was really getting tired of her. At this point, I wanted to put her out of my car. Call Keith and tell him to come pick his pregnant wife up outside of this Walgreens.

"Look, leave me alone, not everyone has the perfect planned out life like you!"

"Perfect? You know more than every other person in my life that there is nothing about it that is perfect. My mom left me and my father when I was four. I met and fell in love with Keith in college and he did the most awful thing to me and yes, I chose to forgive him. Even after that I've had two miscarriages, but I believe that that I'm going to have this baby because I choose to be happy. I'm going to be okay."

I grabbed my friend, who was now crying, and hugged her while wiping her tears. This wasn't about me; she was hurting. I failed to realize that she was going through this. I assured her that she was going to have her baby and that I was going to be right by her side when she does. I told her I hope the baby doesn't cry as ugly as she is right now; which made her laugh. We sat and talked for hours like we use to in the dorm room. She let me know that she had made it three months past the last two encounters, but she still has it on her mind from time to time. I apologized for being selfish and not recognizing that she too is going through tough life situations. I assured her that I heard her and that I will do better at being that for her as she has been for me.   Chrissy ended up staying the night talking as much as she could. She was tired. I could tell because she would doze off mid-conversation and wake up starting a new one. I just participated in every conversation until she finally fell completely to sleep. She is snoring loudly and spread out on my bed with slob coming from her mouth; it reminded me of the first night that we were roommates. We got into the biggest argument. The rooms were small and I was already annoyed with her because she got the side of the room I wanted then ignored the instructions on what not to bring because she brought her entire house with her, making the room even smaller. The first night as roommates, I just could not fall asleep with her snoring so loudly. At first, I kindly tried to nudge her, but she would not move. After about thirty minutes, I threw a pillow at her, and the girl just rolled over snoring more intensely. That was it; I had reached my breaking point and felt hell since she is keeping me from sleeping so I was going to wake her ass up too. So, I got a bottle of water from my mini-fridge and poured the whole bottle on her. She was furious but so was I. We got into a big argument and before you know it, our entire floor was now up and at our door. When I opened the door, she had gotten a full water bottle and threw it at me. Immediately, I turned and pounced over on her, trying to make her wish she had never done that. Luckily, the resident assistant was now there because the other ladies on the floor were all chanting "fight, fight!" The resident assistant was a big lady who was in her senior year; she wore these turtle pajamas bottoms and a dingy t-shirt with some kind of food stain on it. All I could hear is they "don't pay me enough for this shit" as she pulled me off of Chrissy. We got in trouble our first night as college students, and I thought for sure that I would get a new roommate, but to my surprise, she was still in my room the next morning. But after the punishment of sleeping in the room with the RA whose room was beyond junky as fuck then and she snored as well, I figured I could manage my living situation. Besides, there was no way that I was going to try that shit with the RA, I knew better; she would beat my ass, and that was fact.

In the midst of me reminiscing, Chrissy let out a loud snore, and I just started laughing wondering how sweet of a person she is because had the roles been reversed and she did that to me, I don't think I would have forgiven a person that I hadn't known not even for twenty-four hours.

Chapter 13: An Eventful Day

A week had gone by since Chrissy had her meltdown. I'm glad she got to express herself even though she took a few jabs at me that have been on my mind lately. It is funny how you find out how people really feel when they are upset, but I guess I will let it slide this time. Work was a little draining today, but as I was preparing to leave, I reached for my phone out of my purse. Eve has called me four times and sent a message to call her as soon as possible. I quickly pack my things to leave, calling Eve as I was walking out of the office. She is on the phone crying hysterically, and I cannot make any sense out of what she is saying. "Is everything okay!?" After a couple of seconds, she gathers herself, and I can hear her clearly now. I couldn't believe. She said her husband filed for divorce. "This funky bastard is asking for

- My house
- My range rover
- 800 in alimony
- Split custody
- Split all of my bank accounts including my business
- He wants the twins on all holidays."

Then she started to cry again. I have never seen my sister so helpless that I didn't know what to say. She always seemed to have it all together. I tried to act as if I didn't know that they had been separated and asked her, "why is he all of a sudden wanting a divorce?" Not thinking she would actually open up; she spills some news that I didn't expect.

I could not believe what I was hearing. My sister Miss Perfect who has it all together basically shared with me that she had an affair on her husband for over six months and when he found out he moved out. I never thought she would actually cheat on her husband, but I could see that she wasn't attracted to his lack of ambition. My sister is a successful doctor who has her own small practice and was married to a man who basically was a stay-at-home father. Not because he had to be; he was actually very intelligent, but he seemed to have gotten so used to being laid off from his engineering job a year after the twins were born that he never went back to work. I can see how that could be an issue, but I do not understand why miss bossy would not just leave him. My parents and I thought she was going to a few years ago because she treated him horribly; always belittling him around family and friends for not working, but she stayed. Foolishly so did he. It was at the time that he seemed to need her to lift him that she pushed him down so I could see why he got stuck especially not receiving the support from the one person he needed it from the most.

Now, she is on my phone, crying her eyes out to me, and I did not understand why. She was not the kind of big sister that really gave support. She always would put on for my parents like we were really close, but in actuality, she was not pleased that I wanted to be a designer. She felt that it was not good enough, a waste of time and any money. She sometimes talked about my mom having a daycare when growing up as if it weren't enough compared to her standards. So, at this moment, as she is crying to me, I find it hard to be sensitive; I mean she is the one who demanded that they get a pre-nup and it was his money that started her practice. If we didn't know it, she would make it seem as though she didn't get help from her husband and my parents' little daycare to help start her business. I loved my sister, and even though she always had my back, she is Just as much of a jerk over the years, so I did my best not to upset her more, attempting to calm her down. By the time I made it home, she was lucid and calm to think rational. She even admitted that most of this was her fault. I guess when you lose the one you love you really see your wrongdoings in the entire situation. There was a knock at my sisters' door; the twins were home, so we ended our conversation.

I began to clean my house and prepare my dinner for the night. I decided to have a glass of wine to go with my loaded potato soup and lobster tails. Cooking was my hobby. I loved to cook whenever I had free time. Now that I only had this one job working very few hours, I really had time to cook more so I did every night. Most of the times, it is something simple like beans, rice, noodles because money is beyond tight around here, but today I wanted to treat myself. Besides, I will be presenting soon so I will be getting my big check soon. I sit on my black leather sofa, preparing to watch a movie and just chill. I would normally go back to the gym, but I think I will take a break today, but before I could get good into the movie, my phone rang.

Chrissy was in a panic crying saying that she believes the baby is coming and her husband is out of town she asked me to meet her at the hospital. I grabbed my purse, threw on some sweats and a t-shirt then headed to the hospital. I was driving extremely fast. I cannot believe that I did not get a ticket. When I got to the hospital, I checked in to get her room number. Chrissy wasn't due for a few more weeks, so I hope everything is okay. I was extremely nervous heading to her room, but I made sure not to have that on my face when I entered. I was calm and told her that everything was going to be fine, but I have to admit I was really nervous.

Three hours later, my best friend gave birth to a beautiful, healthy baby boy. She didn't want to know the gender prior to birth. They just prayed for a healthy baby. The doctor allowed me to have Keith on Facetime so that he could witness his first child being born. Man, I have to love them because that was the most devastating shit that I had ever seen before. It took everything in me not to pass out. But I was glad that I could be there for my friend and her husband. He profusely thanked me for helping him witness the birth of his first child

Keith Jr. who I have already named KJ. That night, I stayed with her and KJ, by 8:30 the next morning Keith made it, so I left to give them some alone time.

Chapter 14: Presentation Blues

It's been an eventful past couple of days that I forgot for a second to be nervous about my presentation. Ms. Kelly accelerated the presentation date because I had gotten finished early. I was indecisive if I wanted her to change the date or not because, on one hand, I was nervous but then that meant I would get the payment sooner and I sure could use that money right now. Her first intent was only for me to help her during the holidays, which I later found out, but after letting her know that I wasn't working, she did create a position for me. She isn't sure what she will have me do now that I am done, and everyone has returned back to work, but that's the least of my worries right now. The week has come that I have to present, and I am extremely nervous, wondering if I will make sense when I speak. I've put a lot of time, thought, effort, and energy into this presentation that I would hate for them not to like it or not take me seriously being that I was someone who lucked up getting this big responsibility just from responding to an email blast during Christmas break. I hope I sound competent when I present; displaying that I do know. Sometimes my nerves get the best of me, and I stumble over my words, but I really know what I am doing. If only public speaking didn't make me so anxious, I would nail this for sure. I have practiced on Chrissie and Keith, but they are family, so that was easy. It's when I get in front of a crowd of people with their serious, stern looks that make me doubt myself. But I never throw in the towel without trying, so I will do this presentation giving it my best; let's just hope it's good enough. I explained to Ms. Kelly, my fear of public speaking, which made her push me to do it even more, saying that this would be a good experience as well as great exposure. She also thinks it may be what I need to get me out of my comfort zone. I believe that I am up for the task. As I sit at my dining room table with all of my work displayed across, I hear the doorbell ring. I know it is not Chrissy because she is still in the mommy-moon phase and I really do not have any other unexpected company. To my surprise, it was my mother; she has come to be my support system because she knows how nervous I have been about doing this pitch. Needless to say, I was beyond grateful to see her; she did bring a sense of calmness with her. She stayed with me all night and even fixed dinner, which I demolished no one cooks better than my mom.

The next morning, I get up, pull out my navy-blue slacks with the matching blazer, yellow poke-a-dot top that has this cute string bow tie and yellow heels. I loved the beauty of heels, but if it were up to me, I would wear sneakers all the time; they are reliable in most situations. I have my hair in a sleek ponytail to the back; my ponytail was actually a little bushy because I just washed my hair. In the kitchen, my mom fixed a breakfast for a champion; too bad I couldn't eat it; my nerves wouldn't let me. I kept getting that bubbly feeling in my stomach. I gathered my things, and my mom gives me the biggest hug and inspirational speech out the door. It feels good to have her in my corner.

As I stand here in front of all of these strange faces, I attempt to display confidence when I speak. I stumbled a few times at the beginning, but then it began to flow. At the end, it's like the entire room hands went up with questions. To me, this was a great thing because it meant that they were interested, but sometimes there are those who just want to test your knowledge; either way, I was prepared. After I was finished, I went back into the small conference room, and Ms. Kelly came in to congratulate me on a job well done. She and the team were very impressed with my work and loved every design. Ms. Kelly told me that she had some things to finish up out of town and it would take her a few weeks but since I had done such great work to take time off and that we could meet when she returns to discuss future business ventures if I were interested. Curious, I asked, "what kind of business ventures?" "We will discuss that in a few weeks. Your payment for the presentation will be deposited in your account along with this week's pay on Friday. Thank you again for all of your help; you really exceeded my expectations." I displayed a smile that I hadn't been able to do in a long time, and it felt good. I felt good about myself, which is something I cannot say I have done in a while.

I went straight home, telling my mom the good news; I even gave her a little snippet of the presentation that I had just given. I hung out with my mom for the next two days until it was time for her to return home. I walked my mom into the airport and sat with her because she liked to get there extremely too early, so we had lots of time to pass. "Jahiri, so what are you going to do now? I mean I understand that you have a possible situation lined up with your boss but until you find out whatever that is?" "Oh Ma, I just got that $2,000.00 stipend for the presentation, so I'll be alright, besides you know that's just my part-time gig." But it actually wasn't. I was two months behind on my car note and a month behind on my rent. Luckily, I communicate with them or else I would be homeless and carless. This money was going straight towards that. My student loan payment is in forbearance, and luckily, I have been able to pay utility bills. "Well, don't think I was snooping or anything, but I was looking for some lotion the other day, and I saw three past due notices on your dresser. Now don't get mad at me but I looked at them. Before you say a word, I just need to know what is going on and why didn't you feel that you could come to your dad and I for help" "Ma, I am fine; those are old." "Jahiri, don't look at me and lie to my face, that is just disrespectful, and I don't appreci-ate it. I cannot go home, leaving you here knowing that you are here struggling like that." I got a lump in my throat because I wanted to cry, but I held it in. "Well, I lost my job a little before Christmas, but I didn't think it would be this long before I found something else. Ma, I have tried to apply for numerous jobs, but I haven't had any luck. I tried to get a business loan over and over, but I have been rejected each time. I wanted to tell you, but at first, I thought I could fix it myself but then as time passed; I was just too embarrassed. I didn't want you and daddy to be mad at me thinking you wasted your money on my education and I'm not doing anything with it." "We will never think of you as a failure, and out of everyone in this family, we know that you are a hard worker. It is okay to ask for help sometimes don't you know we helped your sister? Even though she tries to proclaim that she did it all by herself, that's not the case. No one can do it all by themselves, and I want you to remember that anytime you are going through anything. If you would have asked for help, you may not have been in this situation. Now I have told your dad so he will be putting some money in your account to help you catch up on your bills." "No, Ma I got it I'll be fine."

As I walked to the car, it's like my emotions took over me because I could not stop crying. There were so many people looking at me that I felt awkward, but for some reason, I just could not stop the tears from falling. When I finally got into the car, the tears flowed even more. I did not understand why this was happening, but it was like that over-whelming feeling took over of me having lost my job; now I am barely making it, depleted my savings and now picking and choosing which bill to pay each month. It is crazy because I hated my job, but it did give me a sense of security, and now I am doing something that I love, but I'm barely able to survive on my own. It is embarrassing that I am twenty-six and my mother is in the airport lecturing me in front of strangers. I feel like a fucking failure …how did I get to this point? I could not figure out what I did to deserve this, and the tears just started falling harder. At this point, my eyes were so big and red with my runny nose. I sat in my car letting those built-up emotions out and be-fore I knew it an hour had passed. In that hour I had time to really think and reflect. I was thinking of calling my mom and taking her up on her offer. I was ready to throw in the towel. I didn't have any more energy in me, and I really need the help. I started my car and put it into gear to leave out of the airport. As usual, traffic was ridiculous, which made it seem impossible to get out into the street. Without thinking clearly, I tried to make a quick turn. I heard a loud truck horn then a big BOOM!!! I could hear faintly "ma'am, can you hear me? Are you okay?" After that, things became very blurry.

Chapter 15: An Unexpected Event

I could hear her voice, but I didn't see her. I had the worst headache in the world. It took about fifty tries to finally get my eyes open. It was like I had been in a long, deep sleep that kind that leaves the hard crust in your eyes. As I finally opened my eyes, I saw a room full of people and right to my side was my mom. I was so confused because I know I just dropped her off. She had been crying, but her smile showed some relief. She started kissing me and praising God. With confusion on my face, I could hear someone calling for the doctor.

The doctor entered the room to speak with me, but for some reason, I couldn't talk when I tried. I grabbed my mother hand to stay with me, and she did just that. He began to explain that I had been in a bad car accident. He further explained that I had a minor concussion, a broken leg with minor bruises and cuts. He assured me that me after running several test; that I was going to be just fine. The doctor let me know that my leg will require extensive physical therapy if I want to properly heal. He provided me all of the documentation and let me know if I do well over the next couple of days, I will be prepared to be discharged from the hospital.

Within those minutes, I had received so much information that I did not know how to process it. My family had come in, and everyone was giving me so much love, I was just grateful to have them and to be alive that I did not really care about anything else. My mom, dad, sister and nephews were there for hours, and I did not want them to leave. The twins were getting restless, so my dad took my sister and nephews to the hotel to get some rest, but my mom stayed with me. About twenty minutes later, Chrissy came rushing in kissing on me and told me to never scare her like that again. We both laughed and began talking. She gave me an update on the baby and told me she would bring him by tomorrow to visit.

Early the next morning, the pushy ass nurses came in, messing with me trying to make sure everything was okay, but I had an attitude, not really up for being nice. After they were done or over my attitude, they left the room, and my mom comes out of the bathroom, saying how rude I was to people who are trying to help me. "I don't know what has gotten into you lately, keeping secrets, being rude. You should be happy to be alive right now." My mom was hurting. The thought of losing her child had to be tough for her to deal with. I felt bad, but I too was hurting, and I was tired of suppressing my feelings to make everyone else happy. I felt a tear fall down my face. "Ma, I cannot even take care of myself, I can't pay my bills, I lost my job, and I am in so much debt right now. I don't know what I am doing down here, but I am not doing something right, and now you're telling me I have a broken leg which means more bills. FUCK, Ma, what am I sup-posed to do?!" Help me. I need help, please help me, Ma. I don't want to be this bitter unhappy rude person. Please help me." I repeated that over and over while she hugged me and rubbed my back while I let all my frustration out.

"you are my daughter, and I raised you to be strong. You may feel defeated, bruised and broken, but you are still here, so you have the opportunity to do something with all of these emotions that you are pouring out right now. The Jahiri I know is a fighter, creator, in-novator, and self-starter. You've been down for a minute, but when you are ready, God will help you get back up. I am always going to help you, no matter the circumstance. As long as I have breath in my body, you never have to question that baby." In that moment, she spoke life into me. Words are powerful, and right now, her words poured strength, encouragement, love, compassion, healing and power into a broken woman. In that moment I recognized that I could no longer be that young girl with an idea of the woman I desired to be, but I actually had to become that woman accepting that it comes with the responsibility dealing with all of the tough situations that life brings my way. My mom was my strength which is something that I have always admired about her. She could make a difficult situation look easy, but I know she too has encountered difficult situations she just did a good job of hiding it from me.

There was a knock at the door. It was the doctor letting us know that my test came back good, and I would be able to go home in a couple of days, but I will need to go to physical therapy for my leg. He informed to be patient, and in due time, the minor cuts and scars will heal. I was excited to be going home because sleep isn't really an option in the hospital with all the nurses coming in and out throughout the day and night. I was over being prinked and poked on; I was ready to go home and grateful that everything is okay.

Chapter 16: Hard times meet Hard times

It has been a few days since I had been released from the hospital. My sister and the twins went back home a few days ago. My mom and dad were still here. My dad had helped me with my finances. The shit was mad embarrassing having my dad go through my bills with me and help me catch up on everything. He even paid my rent up until the end of my lease, which wasn't far away. I didn't have a car note anymore because of the accident, but I was going to be receiving a check, and I decided I was going to use it to buy a cash car for now. Embarrassing as it was; I was truly grateful knowing I had one less thing to worry about. My dad was preparing to leave because now that he was retired; he was really hands-on with my mom's daycares, and he wanted to go back to make sure things were still running afloat. Later that night, my mom left to drop my father at the airport. She was staying with me for a few more weeks which meant until I was able to take care of myself. I took out my laptop to check my email; I missed a lot from Ms. Kelly, but I just opened the most recent one. She had sent a get-well card and flowers to the hospital, so I assumed someone told her about the accident.

Her email went as followed:

Dear Ms. Strong,

I am pleased to share with you that your presentation went extremely well, and now the new product line is preparing to be launched in several of my stores. I really appreciate your hard work and dedication to help bring my vision to life in such a short period of time. I think you would be a great asset to the growing development of this company and I would like to schedule a meeting with you once you have healed to discuss some ideas and opportunities that I have for you with this company. If interested, please reach out to me as soon as you get an opportunity to discuss your thoughts and feedback.

Sincerely,
Ms. Kelly, CEO

I instantly responded to the email to Ms. Kelly neglecting the fact that I cannot do much of anything right now. I just hope she does not change her mind. I was excited to see what she wanted to discuss with me. I started to come up with many scenarios in my head but then stopped, deciding I would just be patient. My thoughts were interrupted by a text alert on my phone. I had not used my phone since I had woken up in the hospital; I am not sure why, but I just had not thought about it. Damn, I am either loved or people are being extremely nosey. The text that I just recently received was from Sabrina. For her choice of words, you would have thought she loved me, but how could that be possible when she went out of her way to hurt me. I wasn't ready to speak with her as she requested that I call her when I feel up to it. Not today, not now I have too much going on to deal with her mess. I missed the person that I thought Sabrina was. I mean the loss of a relationship is hurtful in any form. I had been friends with her for a very long time so the love that I have for her didn't just disappear no matter how hard I tried to make it. I sometimes wanted to call her and ask her what made her want to hurt me out of all people, but then I don't know if I could handle her answer. I don't think there is anything she could say to justify her actions.

Every day started to feel like my life was on repeat. I couldn't do anything, and my leg was in so much pain. I really didn't talk to my mom I just sat in my bed watching Netflix. Ms. Kelly never responded to my email, which really threw me for a loop. She always responds. I guess she got all of the work she needed out of me but she still hadn't cut my insurance off she has me on FMLA but because I didn't make enough for short term disability so now I don't have any income coming in. I was current on all of my bills now, so that wasn't a big deal. I did not have my phone. I cut it off and threw it in my nightstand. I cried at night when my mom was asleep. Chrissy tried to come over but I didn't want to see her. I didn't want to see anyone. I wanted to smile and be happy, but I didn't know how. I was sad all the time. My mom let that go on for about a week until she got fed up with what she called "my pity party" and started getting on my last nerve.

She gets up extremely early playing music making tons of noise. She began to wake me up with her at five in the morning. I wake up; she helps me comb my hair and makes me sit at the table like I am a little girl again; she has me on a real schedule. I thought I was helpless before well now I know things could have been worse. After a while, I began to get used to her schedule, but I still waited for her to wake me. However, this morning my mom tried to wake me up, but I was already sitting up in my bed waiting for her. She tried to comb my hair, but I pushed her off reaching for my products, attempting to do it myself, this was a fail because it was hard trying to maintain balance and comb my hair, so I faked it which reflected in me still having a jacked up ponytail. I then crutched myself to my closet, picked out some sweats and a hoodie. I was able to put my tops on with no help, but I had to ask for help with my bottoms. She had a smirk on her face that annoyed me once I got back up I went to the kitchen, got a box of cereal. It wasn't the one that I wanted, but I wanted to show her that I could do it myself, so I fixed a bowl of cereal for breakfast. Once I was finished, I called my doctor's office and got the information I was supposed to obtain about physical therapy a week ago. I have made a payment plan to pay off my hospital bills which my parents are paying for now. After I finished handling business, I went to the laundry room to help my mom wash clothes. I asked her if she could help put things on lower shelves so that I could reach them to be more helpful around the house. She did just that with no hesitation. I also put my hair products on my dresser since I had a mirror and chair in there; it made it much easier to sit and comb my hair. I was upset with my mother for treating me like a child, but honestly, I was pouting and acting like one. This was an adjustment for me, but I needed her annoying tough love to get me back to reality.

Every morning I started to feel better and stronger. My mom still helped me a lot, and I thanked her as much as possible. She did what she needed to do to show me that I am not helpless; I just had to put effort into doing better, so I did. "Here you go Jahiri; your phone was ringing." "Thanks, Ma." "Hello." "Good Morning Ms. Strong, this is Ms. Kelly, how are you." "I am doing well. How are you?" "I am doing so so, but I was calling to see if you would be willing to begin back working soon? My assistant has been let go, so I really need some help. I will keep your pay at the same rate for a 40 hour per week, but you will be able to make your own schedule I just need you to be available from 8-11 each morning just in case I need you to send an email or two." "Yes, that's fine I will just need whatever it is you will have me working on." Of course, I will get someone to bring you everything. And this will not be a lot of work I know you are still healing. I just trust that you will get the things that I need done. Thank you." I really didn't want to be her assistant, I mean I just presented to investors, and now you want me to be your assistant. Is that what she had in mind when she sent that email? I was irritated, but again, right now, I didn't have time to focus on myself the bigger pitcher was to heal and have some type of income so that I can take some of the extra pressure off my parents. Even though I know it's not pressure on them more so on me so I can stop feeling like a needy 26-year-old dependent.

I was able to get the doctor to provide documentation to return back to work with the stipulations to only work from home with light duty. When it was time for me to begin working Ms. Kelly became ill and was rushed to the hospital. She is in her mid-sixties, but she seemed to be in good health. Maybe all of the stress of work and never taking off has caught up with her, but I wasn't sure. When I found out, I called to check on her, but you would have never known she had been sick because she was still in business mode. She asked me if I would be able to manage the business journals, which included her inventory, sales and profit. She had me doing this a while every-one was out, but that wasn't for long. I told her that I would definitely work on that for her while she was out. She also assigned me to do weekly check-in on her store here in Atlanta via video call so that I could see updates. She is preparing to either close it or turn it into another furniture store, so she wants me to check-in and make sure that they are clearing it out.

Chapter 17: Note to Self

I was quickly learning that managing several businesses was no easy task. I mean going over Ms. Kelly business logs made my eyes cross. I would get confused sometimes and email her to ask questions which I hate doing because she was home trying to get better. But, she always replied quickly or called back to talk me through everything. I learned how to determine if a business is making profit, and I must say this woman is very wealthy. When I first did the video conference call to the store, it was cute but very outdated. I wouldn't dare tell her that though. This store was the only store that wasn't making her any income it actually was costing her more to keep it open than what she profited from it. The workers in the store were always so kind when I called. It was like I was their employer, but I wanted to let them know we had the same boss. I didn't, I kept it professional and gave them weekly updates on what Ms. Kelly wanted them to do. Basically, she decided to close the store and wanted them to clear it out. Once they were finished, she had hired a contractor to remodel the place, and to my surprise, she gave me all creative control over it but to keep the work within the budget that she had set for the renovations. I anxiously waited for the staff to finish up so I could begin to work with the contractor on the design concept I have for this location. Hopefully, I am up and moving by then.

My mom had to go home for a week for work, and I told her that I didn't have anywhere to go this week so I would be fine. She set me up with a kitchen full of groceries, so I felt that I could manage for a week. I also had Chrissy and Keith that I could call to help me if I really needed it. Well, the next morning, after my mom was gone; I hear a noise at my door. I instantly grab my phone, bat and pepper spray off my nightstand. I couldn't move that fast, so I sat up holding my bat like I was at a ballpark waiting for the pitch. The noise stopped, but my heart continued racing then a few moments later, I hear a loud banging on the door. I was freaking out at this point I didn't know what the hell I was going to do. I thought about throwing myself in the closet, but it was so far away. My phone rang, and it was Eve. I immediately answered, but before I could tell her what was going on, I heard her say "damn, come open the door." My heart still pounding I moved as quickly as possible, which was turtle fast to grab my crutches and get up. Hopefully, when I start physical therapy next week, I find out how long I have to wear this damn cast and be on these crutches. When I finally got to the door Eve was laughing holding her phone with her timer showing six minutes and twenty-two seconds. She timed to see how long it would take for me to get to the door. I wanted to smack her in the face with this crutch, but she had the upper hand being that I couldn't bob and move the way I wanted to so envisioned slapping her and it was a little satisfying. Eve walked right past me with her luggage and food she brought from the breakfast spot up the street. I didn't know she was coming and from the stuff she brought I hope she wasn't replacing my mom for too long.

Over breakfast, I learned that my sister volunteered to come help me while my mom was home. I guess Eve has a heart after all. When I finished my work for the day, my sister cooked spaghetti and garlic bread. I did not want to eat it because my sister was a lot of things, but a cook wasn't one of them. The noodles looked mushy, and the ground beef looked bland and undone. So instead of eating the food, I asked her how things were going at home. She smiled and let me know that the twins are doing great and showed me pictures. "Guess what, I am dating someone, and I really like him, but I don't think I am ready to bring him around my kids or the family just yet, but I think he is a good guy. I could tell she was happy because she hasn't been this nice in years. As I was sitting there catching up with my sister, my stomach started to growl, and I remembered the time I stayed over at Eve's house and she attempted to cook chicken, broccoli, and mashed potatoes for dinner. Sitting at the table with my nephews, Zachariah told Zaire not to eat the chicken, and when I asked him why he responded, "granny chicken doesn't have this black stuff on it, so I think mommy got the wrong kind. Don't eat cause you might get sick." Zarie agreed with him. Zachariah had no filter and brutally honest. Now I am sitting at the table laughing and my sister has no clue as to why. I told her I couldn't eat that mess, so I was going to order food. She quickly jumped on board, putting her order request in throwing out our plates.

Over the next few days, Eve went out shopping and brought me back something each time she went. She loved to shop, and I enjoyed the gifts. Because there is such a huge age gap between us, she always spoiled me as if I were her child before she had the twins. I wasn't as mobile and getting in and out of a car was very hard, so I stayed home, but she would facetime me to see if I liked the items before purchasing. I ended up with three new sweatsuits, a couple of t-shirts, and a pair of gym shoes. Today was such a beautiful day for March in Atlanta, which, to Eve, felt like summer, so she was really enjoying herself. I pulled out my sketchbooks for the first time in a very long time, one was filled with sketches of shoes and the other was filled with women clothing. It was approaching a year since I received my MBA, and I hadn't made any progress to owning a store or even developing a line. I honestly hadn't put in any work towards it since I lost my job several months ago. I'm not even sure if I should be pursuing this anymore, maybe my sister was right, and this should just be a hobby or a hustle to make extra cash. I honestly don't know what I am supposed to be doing anymore, and I hadn't gotten any calls for job interviews, but, at this point, no one will probably want to hire me because I cannot really work until after I complete physical therapy. I never imagined that this is how things would work out for me. I haven't told anyone, but I am really considering moving back home with my parents until I figure things out. I know people will have things to say, but it might be what happens when my lease is up.

I initially pulled out my sketchbook because I made a promise to Chrissy years ago that when she has her first child, I would design the baby custom pieces for a photoshoot well, she called me up the other day, reminding me of that promise. I told her that I would. Chrissy put in a request for a top for herself as well. She was going to purchase all of the material that I needed, so I had nothing to worry about. I didn't have much to do, and I loved my new nephew, KJ, who looks more like he should have been named Chrissy Jr. As I flipped through a few more pages, an old picture of me sitting at my grandmother's sewing table fell out.

On the back was a message I wrote to myself for a class project when I was probably in the eighth or ninth grade that said:

Remember your dream, then set goals to achieve it!

Future

Designer -J. Strong

This reminds me of that H.E.R. song, <u>*Sometimes,*</u> I heard the other day, and I began to cry. That song said it best, and right now, I am living that truth. It's funny how as a kid, you are so filled with joy, passion, motivation, drive that you think you can accomplish whatever you set out to do, never considering that life isn't always so beautiful and filled with happy endings. I wiped the tears off my face because I didn't want Eve to catch me crying. I didn't feel like trying to explain myself because she wouldn't understand. After I cleaned my face, I began working on a design for an outfit for KJ, by the time Eve came home, I had three and a half sketches. I was in a zone and designing baby clothes was something I had never done but was very thrilling to me, which I didn't expect. The sun was going down, and it was getting cool outside, so I went into the house. Eve brought home some *Papadaux*, which was our favorite, so I was prepared to feast on the food. She even brought a bottle of wine, and since I wasn't taking pain medicine right now, I got a glass. As we're sitting on the couch eating,
Eve started talking
     "So, what are your plans for your birthday next month?"
     "I honestly hadn't put much thought into it with all that is going on."
     "Understandable, but you only get one birthday, and you have a lot to be thankful for this year little girl, you almost lost your life in that car accident."
     "True, and I am grateful to be alive, but that doesn't mean I have to do anything big, and besides, right now, there isn't much that I can do in this situation."

"Well, is there anything you want for your birthday?"

"No, not really, and besides, you can say the things you bought me this week are for my birthday. Not to mention you coming down to help me out. I really appreciate that. I think that's enough."

"Girl, if I wanted to gift you something for your birthday, it wouldn't be no damn sweatpants. So, what do you want for your birthday since we aren't traveling or having a party?"

"My own store, Money to develop my line. Yeah, that's what I want for my birthday" I said this to shut her up and it worked.

"Aw hell, well, forget it then. So, you didn't tell me that Chris was not the father of Sabrina baby".

"I didn't know that to tell you."

"Oh shit, I thought you would have forgiven her by now like always, but I guess you are really done with her this time. Well, girl, hell yea. Her mom told Ma how he came over to the house, cutting up on Bri cussing her out for lying. I wonder if she knew all along that wasn't his baby but hell who cares that's her mess to figure out".

I didn't say a word. I continued to eat my food because that exactly how I felt it was her mess to figure out and me talking about her no matter how mad I am at her really wouldn't make me feel better. She was once my friend, and I loved her like family, so I am not going to put her down now. I pray she finds whatever it is she is looking for, but I am not reaching out to her trying to save her anymore. I have to focus on me right now, and I have a lot of shit to figure out, so Sabrina and her drama was not on my list of things to discuss. Luckily, Eve's phone rang, and it was the twins. Eve answered the phone, and I could hear Zachariah yelling, "mom, when are you coming home?! Paw Paw done put us out again. He said we talk too much". We both laughed. My dad put them out of the house every time they were over. Not really, but he threatens to kick them out thinking they would act right, but it never really worked because they knew my mom would never go for that. Eve let the boys know she would be picking them up from school tomorrow afternoon, and from the screams, they were happy.

As Eve finishes her glass of wine, she picks up my sketchbook begins to go through them. She doesn't say a word; she just looks with a neutral face. I try to pretend as though I am not trying to read her thoughts, but I am. She was hard to read; if I ever get her approval on anything other than working in a company using my business degree, I'd be in utter shock because she thinks my passion is a hobby that doesn't promote sustainability. When she gets to the work that I had been playing around with for KJ she puts a big smile on her face, and I hear her say, "Jahiri, now this is some nice work when are you going to put this out?" "Oh, that's just something that I am doing for Chrissy's son, KJ, nothing major." "Well, if you are this creative with something that you are making for your godson, then I can only imagine if you made this a line. I mean, this logo is beautiful and can be used for boys' and girls' clothing. It's also a great market being that there are millions of babies born every day. Have you ever thought about creating a baby clothing line?" "I actually haven't. I have been so fixated on a shoe boutique that I really had not thought about anything else. I love to create clothes, but I never got any compliments on my work besides family, so I never really thought about putting my efforts into that field." "You really should consider it; I think you would truly succeed." Before I knew it, Eve had pulled out my laptop and started researching the baby clothing market. Eve is brilliant, and research is her life. She always says to be the best; you have to be open to learning, which reflected. I was amazed at all of the things that we gathered that afternoon. By the end of the night, she created me a spreadsheet with tips on the target of items I would need to make, how I would make a profit, essential baby items, and much more. I was amazed at how she could capture that information so quickly. I had taken a business class, but it was a struggle for me the entire journey I just knew that it was some information that I needed to be a successful business owner and I believe that to be true because it taught me a lot, but that doesn't take away the fact that those classes were tough. At the end of the night, before I went to bed, I hugged Eve tightly. It was my way of saying thank you for coming to spend time with me because I needed you. When I finally let go, she grasped the message behind my hug, and as she walked out of my room with a smile on her face, I heard her say, "I love you too."

The next morning my sister gathered her bags, which were double what she came with. She had to borrow one of my suitcases because she bought so much stuff while she was shopping this week. When Eve left, she told me to think of something that I wanted for my birthday and let her know. When she arrived, I wasn't excited at all, but right now, I am sad that she is leaving. I would never tell her that. I think she kind of knew because she said she would be back soon to visit or when I am back up and moving; we can go on a trip. I locked the door behind her; since I had nothing to do, I began trying to sew one of the sketches I had for KJ with some scraps that I have from the last shirt that I made. Chrissy is going to bring over the fabric and material I need this week. When my phone rang, it was Eve letting me know that she had made it home. I didn't realize that I had been working that long. She didn't stay on the phone long just to let me know that she had made it.

Chapter 18: Check-Up

It was finally time for my check up on my leg, so I was up this morning like it was the first day of school. I hadn't been out of the house in weeks, and I was ready to go. I put on my grey, and black Nike sweats with a black cropped tank top. Eve bought this outfit for me last week, and I freaking love it. It's so comfortable because she got the pants perfectly oversized, which made it a breeze to put on over this cast. Eve washed my hair and did a braid out for me when she was here. Since I hadn't been anywhere, that is how I wore it for the past couple of days. Because I wanted to be semi-cute today, I did my make up and took my braids out. My hair had grown to bra length now. Sabrina and I decided that we were going to go natural the summer before our senior year. I wanted to transition, but she was so hyped to just cut it all off, so one day, we made a pact that we would cut it off. Well, after we hyped ourselves up; I went home and immediately went to my mom restroom to get her hair scissors. I went to the bathroom and cut all of my hair off just enough for a tiny fro. I cried like a big baby screaming for my mom, who was pissed because I did it without asking her permission. She took me to the beauty shop to get it fixed. After my beautician trimmed it evenly and faded it, making my curls show, I thought I was the finest thing walking. I had a new type of confidence. Well, when Sabrina came over the next day, she still had all of her permed hair and was shocked that I actually went through with it. She hated when school started back, and I received compliments on it, but she never made the transition because she was obsessed with having long hair. Well, I loved it until I grew out to that awkward length, so I wore braids most of that time, but overall, I'm glad I did it. I love the flexibility of being able to have curly hair, big hair, or straight when I wanted to. My go-to hairstyle is big and curly or a ponytail to the back; you could never go wrong with those styles.

As I enter the living room, I hear my mom dancing and singing to my dad. I know they were happy to see each other last week. That's another reason I wanted to hurry up and heal, so my mom could go back and be with my dad. No matter how much I would tell her that I could manage, she is not going to leave until I am off these crutches, and I have not been cleared to drive yet either. Well, hopefully, I am cleared to start physical therapy as planned this week. My dad must saw me creep by because I hear him yell out my name. I walk over to the phone and say good morning watching him attempt to make breakfast which is coffee, fruit, and some muffins that my mom must have prepped for him last week. He was the grill master, but cooking, he stayed away from. I know he missed my mom preparing him meals, but he would never say it. I get my stubborn ways from my father; we will try to figure things out forever before asking for help. Sometimes it's a good thing, but most of the time, it just creates more of a burden than needed. As I walk away, I hear my dad, "babygirl, I put some money in your account this week so you can pay for your doctor visit and physical therapy" "thank you, daddy, I got the alert this morning." "you're welcome, I probably come down there for your birthday, you're getting old can't believe my baby is about to be twenty-seven." "You don't have to come down, daddy, I don't have any plans this year. I think this will be a chill birthday for me. Besides, you and mom have done so much already I don't need anything else." "Well, then I may just come to spend time with my wife since you don't want to see your dad." "I didn't mean it like that; I would love for you to come." His phone paused when he returned letting us know that Zachariah was calling so he would call us back.

When we pulled up at the doctor's office, we sat and waited for about five minutes before they called us back. When I first spoke with the nurse, I asked if I would be getting out of this cast today. She laughed and said it would be up to the doctor. After looking at X-rays, I was cleared to get out that ugly cast, which was replaced with a big, fat uglier boot. I wanted to be done with it all, but at least now, I can take this boot off and scratch my leg and wash it. I was given a list of things that I still needed to do and things to avoid, to continue the progression of healing of my leg. My mom listened and gathered everything as she had done when I was a kid. I was cleared to start therapy this week. The doctor told me it may be hard somedays, but I should push myself so that I can get off these crutches. That was all the motivation I needed!

My mom was calmer now that I was now in this boot, so I asked her if could go out for lunch if I promised to keep my foot elevated at the restaurant. She hesitated, but she agreed. When we got to the restaurant, there was no wait being that it was a weekday, and mostly everyone was at work. We were seated quickly. Because it was a beautiful spring day, we sat outside. The waitress brought over an extra chair for my leg without me asking. She exuded great customer service. "So, Ma, how has it been for you not being at work every day?" "Oh, I have been enjoying myself. I was telling your dad the other day how I think I am ready to retire. He doesn't believe me, but I think I am ready." "Really, I never thought I would hear you say that." "Yes, I think I am so I can travel more and do some of the things that I have put on hold. I have raised my kids, and you both are doing well, and we are financially set. I think I am going to keep ownership and promote directors to complete the day-to-day work so I can enjoy my later years." "I think that would be nice, mom; I think that's what dad has been waiting for." "Yes, I think so too. I'm going to announce it once I go back home so everyone can find out from me and I will move forward from there." "That sounds like a plan, Ma, retire and do your thang gurl!" We both laughed as the waitress walked up bringing our drinks. After lunch, my mom drove me around for a short period just because she could tell I was not ready to go home just yet. I enjoyed being out of the house.

Later that night, I finished sketching some designs for my new baby clothing line. Eve's excitement excited me, so I really got into it. I have sketched baby blanket, onesies, shirts, pants, and socks. Today, I think I want to come up with ideas for bibs. My new plan is to create sketches, sew prototypes of each one, and then have family and friends vote on the best items. Once I gather the numbers, I will develop a proposal that I plan to present to Ms. Kelly to see if she would be willing to invest in my clothing line. I have connections with some of the vendors that she has already introduced me to. I strongly hope she likes my ideas and sees it as a good investment. I continue to re-search so that when I present my proposal, I feel confident in what I am talking about. I haven't told anyone my plans; I think this helps eliminate the pressure of the question "so when are you going to lunch your line" or "dang, you still haven't finished yet" I don't want that pressure anymore, so I am going to move at my own pace and not have any outside pressure. I get a text from Chrissy that she and KJ will be stopping by to visit me this weekend. I immediately shoot her a text back…okay, sis.

Chapter 19: Falling

Sitting in the waiting area at the physical therapy office, I ate my apple and blueberry muffin I brought from home, waiting until they call my name. I finished my breakfast just in time when this petite little woman called my name. She introduced herself as Dr. Breon but informed me that I could call her Dr. Mel or Mel, which is short for Melody. Dr. Mel appeared to be in her early forties, but I could tell that she worked out daily, if not several times a day. She gave me the rundown of what we would be doing and what to expect out of physical therapy. Her first disclaimer was that it is not going to be easy, and it is okay to cry but to keep pushing so that I could heal my leg and get it back fully functioning. Today, I put my all into therapy, but there were many times that I wanted to say "fuck it" walk out and be satisfied with my crutches and this boot. I was now in so much pain. I took as much as I could until I had to ask Dr. Mel to give me a second. She gave me a break letting me know that I was doing a good job. I didn't feel like it. How could simple stuff like bending and stretching my leg hurt so badly? I can only imagine how this is going to go for the next several weeks. I tried not to think about it. Time went by pretty quickly, and I was finished for the day. I told my mom she could run errands while I was here because I didn't mind waiting if I finished before her. I wish I hadn't said that. All I wanted was a Tylenol and my bed. I was trying to hold my jacket and the paperwork Dr. Mel had given me and walk on the crutches to the lobby. When I finally made it to the lobby area, my jacket and paper fell. I was frustrated. I attempted one more time to get my things from the ground when I lost my balance. Before I could fall completely on the ground, a strong arm grabbed me, saving me from falling and total embarrassment. I am so glad the lobby was empty but I'm pretty sure when they look at the cameras, someone will have a good laugh. The man helped me get my things off the ground and helped me sit. "Now stop falling all over the place, your act like your leg is broke or something. Hi, I'm Landon. Here are your things." "Thank you." I attempt to put a smile on my face, but I am in pain, so I really don't know if I was actually smiling or frowning. My mom walked in, looking as if she had interrupted our conversation, but we hadn't had the opportunity to begin one. Landon spoke to her as she walked over to help me. I gave her my jacket and paperwork to hold so

I could get up. "Thank you again, Landon." "You're quite welcome." "So, who is Landon? He sure is one sexy chocolate young man." "I'm not sure, he just popped up when I was falling, trying to grab my jacket and paperwork off the ground." "Ha!Ha! Oh, that's really nice of him. He probably noticed your nice little butt in those yoga pants." "It does look good in these pants, doesn't it? Haha" In my mind, I started to think of how I really looked today. I was semi-cute before physical therapy, but afterward, I was a little worn out. I pulled the visor down to check out my face and hair. I still looked decent. Hell, I don't know why I even cared; I probably never see him again. He didn't appear to be a patient or staff from what I could tell. I stopped thinking about that sexy superhero when I saw the beauty supply store. I asked my mom if she could stop because I had been running low on hair products. I loved to shop and being that I hadn't been able to in a while. I wanted to take my time, but my leg was still throbbing, so I grabbed a few essentials, and then I decided to grab a few boxes of hair dye. Before going into the store, I had no intention of dying my hair, but I had been thinking about a change for a while, so I got it just in case.

When we arrived home, we were met by the delivery man standing outside my door with a bouquet of roses. My dad had sent them to my mom with a note that read: Evelyn, I was sitting here thinking about you, so I decided to send you some roses. I loved how he always did small things to make my mom smile after all these years. She loved it; she called him before getting into the house good. I took my things to set them on the dresser, finally throwing away the hair pudding container that was empty about a week ago. It's something about getting to the end of your favorite hair product and not having a backup that you will rub and scrape the hell of the container, hoping and wishing you can get just a little more in one of the cracks.

After the Tylenol I took in the car started to help the pain, I went to the kitchen and began cooking dinner for the night. My mom was still in the living room on the phone with my dad flirting like she was dating again. The twins taught them how to use their facetime, and they use it every chance they get. I was in the kitchen, blasting my music and cooking when my phone rings. I didn't feel like talking right now, so I waited for it to stop so my music could continue playing, but it rang again. When I get over to my phone, it was Zarie, "Auntie, look what I made you at school today!" "Wow, that's beautiful, what is it?" "It's a toothbrush holder; you can put it in your bathroom." "I sure can thank you for making that for me. Zachariah snatches the phone "Auntie, may I come to your house? When will you know how to walk again?" I attempted to answer him, but as soon as he gets a glimpse of my mom walking in the kitchen, he begs her to take the phone. I wonder if there is a such thing as a grandma boy because he would definitely fit the description. I loved them both, but Zarie was so laid back and chill we had an instant connection. He was also very creative and liked to make things. I want him to see what Chrissy does for a living because I think he will love it. If I knew where I would be this summer. I would see if he could spend a day of work with Chrissy. Maybe I will ask her just in case; I will ask her this weekend.

Chapter 20: A Cry For Help

I straighten up a little before Chrissy and KJ arrive. My mom decided to use the day to go shopping and just enjoy this beautiful Saturday. She asked me to come, and any other time, I would be down for a good shopping day, but Chrissy already made plans to come over, so I didn't want to flake on her she really hasn't been around much lately, so I needed to see her. I can't wait to hold KJ. He is still in that adorable phase where he is loving and sweet. When he gets to be my nephews' ages, I brace myself for what will come out of their mouths. I look at the time it's now 1:35 p.m., Chrissy said she would be over at 11 this morning. She is never late for anything, but she does have another person to get ready now, so I call her. When she answers, she sounds lethargic and drained. I asked her if she forgot about coming over this weekend, and she had. She hurried off the phone and said she will be over shortly. About thirty minutes later, Chrissy knocks at the door. No smart comments or extra smart comment today. I guess she is tired. When I open the door, Chrissy looks bad. She has on a dingy black t-shirt, raggedy yoga pants that have bleach stains, and her hair looks like it has been combed in a while. Her eyes were red and puffy like she hasn't slept in weeks. She tried to force a smile on her face as she hugged me walking in the house. Chrissy is an upbeat, always happy dressed up woman. I mean, she is the only one I know who wears heels every day unless she just has to wear flats. I take the baby from her, and she immediately flops on the couch.

"You look good, Jahiri" "Thanks, so do you." "Oh, you don't have to lie to me. I haven't put on any clothes or touched my hair in weeks. I'm drained. I never knew being a mother would be so hard. I mean, I've wanted a baby for so long, and now that I have one, I just wish I could go back one more day and not have such big responsibility." As she begins to cry, I walk over to hug her because she seems to be having a meltdown again. "I love KJ, Hiri, but you know I didn't know it would be so hard. He cries all night, and because Keith is still working, I take on most of the responsibility so he can rest throughout the night. I wanted to breastfeed, and I did for a while, but it became overwhelming. Now I feel horrible because I want to supply food for my baby, but it is taking the life out of me. Maybe this is why my mom left me with my dad to raise because it was just too hard for her." I sat there holding my friend, who clearly was going through postpartum along with other issues of her past. She really needed help. I tried to comfort her and let her know that everything would be alright. "Have you thought about going back to counseling?" "No, I didn't think I needed to back then when you all persuaded me to go." "Well, remember how you were so sad when you lost the baby? When you started going to counseling, you began to heal and feel better, didn't you?" "I guess. I was hurt back then because Keith cheated on me when I needed him the most. I think that's why I had a breakdown." "But during that crisis, you were able to go to counseling and have a professional help you process your emotions, which helped you walk through them, right?" "Yes…it did." Chrissy cried some more. I took the baby and laid him down, sat Chrissy at the table, made her some food, and made her eat. She ate her food, but when KJ began to cry, she jumped to go get him; I had to force her to sit down, and I went to cater to the baby so she could enjoy her meal. After she ate, I washed my friend's hair and combed it for her. She talked my ear off like normal, which made me happy. After I finished, we sat on the couch to watch tv, but Chrissy instantly fell asleep. I put a cover on her and let her sleep. KJ woke up, so I fixed him a bottle and fed him. He ate, giggled, pooped, and went back to sleep.

Hours later, Chrissy woke up, and she looked refreshed. She went to the bathroom, and when she came back, she just gave me a big hug. "Jaihiri, thank you so much for always being there for me when I need you the most. I didn't want to bother you with all that you have been going on, but unlike you, I need to talk to someone when I am going through things to keep me from going insane. You've always been that person for me, and when you cannot help, you always try to find ways to help me get the help I need. I am going to make an appointment with my counselor this week because you are right; I do need help getting through this, and I still get sad about my mother passing away when I was a kid. I miss her because I didn't get the full experience of being taught how to be a mother. My father was good, but he is a man, and I know sometimes it was tough on him trying to do it all alone, which is why I am also going to allow Keith to help out more because I cannot do it on my own." "Don't ever think that you cannot talk to me no matter what you think I am always here for you." "I know, but this is just the first time in life that I have ever seen you go through so much, and I felt like I needed to be strong for you for a change. I guess you are the strong one in our relationship." Chrissy laughed as she hit me on the arm a little too hard because I tripped a little bit. Kj started to make whining noises, so Chrissy went over to get him, she loved her baby; I never doubted that. That is why I know she needs help processing things right now because it is unlike her to say something like that. "Hey, I am sorry for all that shit I said to you when I was pregnant about you playing it safe. I actually think it takes more courage to try to start a business than just working for a company, and if you felt that you needed more income at the time, that is fine. I mean, I watched you try over and over for a business loan, all while trying to get an actual designing company that you were working for, so I shouldn't have said that. You have worked really hard, and it was wrong of me to say that to you. Sometimes it makes me a little jealous because you are a self-starter." "What do you mean?" "I have always admired how you are independent, always fighting for what you want. I couldn't imagine trying to do it all on my own because Keith is my rock." It is hard, and I wanted to tell her that I was considering moving back home until I got back on my feet, but she is already going through enough I just couldn't put that on her right now. "Thanks for apologizing, sis, we both have qualities that each other admire about one another, but we help each other be better in all aspects of life, so that's all that matters. Love you, guuurl!"

A few hours after Chrissy left my house, I received a text from Keith:

"…thanks sis, my wife was really having a hard time, and I am glad you got her out of the house today. If you wouldn't mind, could you babysit KJ tomorrow so that I can take her out to do something special?"

He already knew the answer, but I hit him back and let him know that I definitely could do that for him. I am so glad Keith is her husband. He has definitely grown into a good man, husband and now father. I love the two of them together.

Fuck, with all that went on today, I didn't even get to give Chrissy the clothes that I made for KJ well I guess he will get them tomorrow. He has gotten kind of chunky; I hope he can still fit them. My mom walked in, interrupting my thoughts with bags of stuff. Eve and I get our shopping habits from our mother. My dad would cringe at the bags that she is bringing into the house right now. I hope she is driving back home because her luggage will be through the roof.

Chapter 21: Me Time

I have absolutely nothing to do today; I am bored as fuck right now. My mom has gotten used to the idea of leaving the house, so today she has gone to get a massage. She is definitely ready for retirement because I haven't seen her do this much for herself my entire life, but she deserves it. I just wish she would have invited me to go with her. I am over being in this house; I feel like I am on punishment for something that I didn't intentionally do. My mom will be gone all day, so maybe I should call an Uber…but I don't feel like dealing with the hassle of getting in and out with my crutches. I am going to walk to the park up the street. Yeah, I think that is what I will do, it is not too far.

As I walk to the park on these crutches, I started to regret my decision, but because I can actually see the swings now, I just continue. Besides, I really needed the exercise, the only thing that I have really been doing is lifting weights, but to my surprise, I haven't gained any weight. When I walk over to the park, there are a few families with there kids playing, but the swings are empty, so I go to the closet one, place my crutches on the ground and sit on the swing. This was a good idea. "You can't go across the monkey bars faster than me." "Bet I can!" Two little boys were in competition across from me. It was so adorable because neither one of them actually made it across but were arguing about who did the best. "Did you fall and break your leg" a little girl with three pigtails and several bows on her head walks up and asks me. "No, I was in a car accident." "Like a car hit you, and you flew up in the air?" "No, not quite like that, haha." "I am so sorry, ma'am. She loves to talk, asking every question that comes to her head." "It is okay." The little girl waves bye as she walks off with her mom. It feels so good out here so peaceful even with all of the noise of the kids playing in the background. I sat for about an hour, just focusing on nothing; just enjoying time. On my walk back to the house, I had the bright idea not to only create baby clothing but to increase it to toddlers as well. I think that would complete my entire collection. I am not going to talk myself out of this; I am going to go for it. I have been battling with the possibility of hearing no again, but at this point, I have nothing else to lose. Besides, if I don't, I will probably regret it, and I don't need that on my plate as well. I am launching a kids' clothing line. I continued to hype myself up as I continued on to the house.

When I get back on my street, I notice my mom's car is not in the driveway, so I don't have to hear her mouth. I grabbed the mail out of the mailbox which no longer makes my head hurt anymore because all of my bills were current. When I get into the house, I place the mail on the table, go to the kitchen, grab a bottle of water and an apple. I wasn't that hungry even though I haven't eaten anything today. I pull out my laptop to document my ideas before I forget them. I also pulled out my sketchbook to come up with some more sketches, but I really do not have anything in my mind to sketch at the moment, so I put that to the side until I come up with an idea. I walk into the living room, cut on the TV, and there is nothing on. I cannot believe cable is so high, and they play the same shows over and over again. I cut the TV off, deciding to go sit on the deck, and as I walk out, I notice my talkative ass neighbor so I tried to sneak back in, but she spotted me. "Hey, girl, I haven't seen you in a long time. I am glad to see you are doing well after the accident. I noticed your mom is still here. Girl, that is good because my trifling ass momma would not stop her life to help me if I needed it." "Hey, girl, how have you been?" "I am doing good, my kids gone with their daddy, so I have the house to myself, so I am over here drinking on some wine just enjoying the day. You want some I can bring some over there to you." "No, thanks, I am okay. Hey, but I have to go check on my food; I just came out for a second. Enjoy the rest of your day." "Okay, girl, I will." She holds up her wine glass as if she were making a toast. I walk in back in the house again with nothing to do, so I go through my mail.

I cannot believe this. A bright yellow envelope addressed from Sabrina. She hates writing, so she really must want me to know whatever it is that was on her mind. The crazy thing is I thought about her the night when Chrissy went on her spill, and I wanted to pick up the phone to call her, but I just couldn't do it. I just wanted to know what made her do what she did and if she really saw me as her friend. I sit down at the table and open up the envelope. It was a card that said I am sorry. I open it up and she has written a lengthy message.

Dear Jahiri,

I hope all is well. I know you I am the last person that you want to hear from, but I needed to express this to you before too much time has passed. I apologize for making up a lie trying to hurt you, but the truth of the matter is that I was hurt. I have been hurting for a long time. Well, when you were here, you were the one person that I could always depend on to be there for me, and sometimes I took advantage of it. You know I have been messed up ever since my dad left and my mom remarried, I was always treated like the ugly stepchild even by my own mother, and I just didn't know how to properly deal with that growing up, so I acted out. Well, when you left for college, I felt abandoned again, and then you made new friends, so I knew you were not coming back. I always felt like I was competing for your attention, but I now know that was all something that I was making up in my head. I wanted our friendship to get back to the way it used to be, and I needed a change, so I moved down there not really to finish school but to get my friend back. Crazy, right? Well, it's true, but when I got there; I knew things would never be the same, and the bond that you shared with Chrissy made me jealous even after all that you did for me. I just couldn't get over my jealousy so when I went back home; I saw Chris at the party, and I was drunk I mean too drunk, so I did something that I regret. I came on to him and caused a big mess between him and his fiancé, but most of all, I made you feel that I had done something with someone that I know you once loved. I started the lie out of anger, but my pride kept me from telling the truth, and I wanted to hurt you the way I felt you hurt me when you left and moved on with your life. Well, my father reached out to me shortly after having my baby because he found out what happened. To make a long story short, I have been going to counseling, and I am fucked up Jahiri, I was dealing with the abandonment issues of my father leaving during my childhood that I was displacing those issues out on you which was detrimental on our friendship from the start. I am sorry, so sorry because you have been a good friend to me even when I didn't deserve it. I know we may never be friends again, but I needed to share that with you. I love you always and wish you the best in life. Oh, and Happy Early Birthday...Xoxo-Sabrina

She enclosed a picture of a beautiful baby girl. I had a lot of emotions after reading her letter. I was sad that it took for this to happen for her father to come back into her life but also happy that it happened so that she could finally get the help that she needed. This situation made her lose a friend, but she gained a beautiful baby girl and the one relationship that she has desired the most, and that's with her father. I hope everything works out for her because she has all the potential to be a great person. She just has some things to work out, but don't we all? I am happy that she sent this letter because I would have let years go on, not addressing the hurt that this broken relationship has caused me. I needed this closure, and I wanted it I just didn't know how to do it, so I am happy that she took it upon herself to continue to reach out to me and provide me with the answers that I have needed since I found out about this entire situation. Damn, life is crazy.

"Jahiri! Hey baby, I am back. Are you hungry? If so, let's go out to eat tonight. I don't feel like cooking." "Hey Ma, yes, I am let me throw on a better shirt." "Okay, I am going to put this stuff up I just bought, and we can leave out. In the car, my mom was jamming to some oldies and trying to sing along with the artist but doing a horrible job. Once her song goes off, and a commercial comes on, I decide to tell my mom about the letter. "Hey Ma, guess what? Sabrina sent me a letter?" "Oh, wow, you are just now getting it?" "You knew she was sending it?" "Well yes, your father told me she came by the house about a month and a half ago asking for your address because you were ignoring her calls. She apparently tried to get it from Eve, but she wouldn't give it to her. But when she started to talk with your father, he really felt bad for her and gave in; besides, he felt that you could do what you please with the letter, but it would allow Sabrina to explain her behavior." "Ma, back when we were kids, I didn't know that her father leaving her would cause her so much pain, but now that I am older, I get it. I would be devastated, had dad walked out on us like that. And when Sabrina's mom finally got her life back on track, she did treat Sabrina differently than her new kids, which is why I think she now tries so hard to make things right with her by overcompensating her with gifts." "You were a kid, it wasn't your place to understand that, and it wasn't for Sabrina's either, but it would have benefited her had she gotten professional help back then, which isn't her fault either, but I am glad that she is getting it now. Carrying all of that pain around for so long had to be weighing her down." "Do you think I should forgive her for what she did, Ma?" "What do you think?" "I would want her to forgive me if the roles were reversed." "Well, go with that." "But I don't think I could ever be her friend again. I don't think that is repairable, but I do forgive her." "That sounds fair to me." It's like I knew that I wanted to forgive Sabrina, but I wanted to tell someone, and Chrissy wouldn't have had anything nice to say about her, so it would have been pointless to bring it up to her. Maybe one day, I will reach out to her, but right now, I am content with the letter that she sent.

Chapter 22: Birthday Ready

I was at another physical therapy session, and the past few that I have come to, I still hadn't run into nor seen Landon. I could tell I was getting stronger because therapy was getting easier while getting more motion back into my leg. Today was family day at the office because I saw a few people with their kids. I thought that was cool; this is not something I witnessed families doing growing up. They weren't out on the floor where the patients were, so it was alright. I met Dr. Mel's two young girls. She mentioned their names, but I can't recall them, but I know that eleven-year-old was a handful, but Dr. Mel gave her a look, and she got her act together. For her to be a tiny woman, she really did demand authority in her demeanor. I finished up all of the tasks that Dr. Mel had planned for me today; she let me know that by next week, I will be off of the crutches and only in the boot for the reaming of the time. I was excited. I learned my lesson from my first visit, so I had a backpack with all of my things in it. When I was finished, I grabbed my bag which didn't have anything but my wallet, jacket, and phone in it. As I sat to tie my shoe, I saw Landon through the glass doors that lead to the floor where we do physical therapy. I had been taking the extra time to make sure I was super cute just in case I saw him here again. My heart was racing fast, hoping that he recognizes me. I see him walk over to Dr. Mel's daughter and give them a hug, and then she walks over and gives him a hug. Fuck, is he Dr. Mel's husband?! Shit, I think he saw me looking over there. I grab my bag and move as fast as I possibly could to get out of there. In the car, my heart was still racing. I felt so bad. Dr. Mel was such a sweet woman, and I was checking out her husband. I feel like a slut. I would have never known he looks to be around my age, but that doesn't mean anything. I couldn't tell anyone, not even Chrissy; I am so embarrassed. Hopefully, I will be done with physical therapy in a few weeks, so I don't have to see her anymore because I just feel horrible, and I was only looking at the guy.

My mom and I decided to go grocery shopping after leaving physical therapy. When we pulled up, we decided to go into Home Goods before going grocery shopping. Needless to say, I bought a new cover for my couch to match the pillows that I was gifted by Ms. Kelly that I helped design. I wanted this beautiful soft rug that my mom picked out, but it wasn't on sale, so I wasn't getting it. We put our bags in the car and headed into the grocery store. They have those motor chairs that I utilized every time we went grocery shopping. We got all of the items we needed and more for a couple of weeks, but truthfully, when we get home, we will remember that we forgot something. I think I should start making a grocery list and actually stick to it. On the way home, we stopped and grabbed food, which didn't make sense since we had a car full of groceries. For some reason we didn't go in we sat in the car at the restaurant and ate our food. I think my mom was hungry the way she devoured her burger.

When we finally made it home and put our things away, I got in the shower. When I got out, I had a missed call and text from Chrissy, letting me know that she had gone to counseling today, and she thinks she will continue at least for a while. I was glad to receive that message. I put some comfy clothes on, then pulled out my laptop to work on my proposal, which I was preparing to present to Ms. Kelly in the near future. I pulled out my old proposal that I wrote years ago when I was in undergraduate school; looking at it now; it was trash. I guess it was good back then, but it didn't have all the key elements to sell my current ideas, and it was not for the same reason, so instead of revamping it, I will just write a new one. So, I took out my note pad and began outlining my ideas.

I created a pretty decent outline if I must say so myself. Once I finished working on my proposal for a couple of hours, I went to the living room where my mom is now in her red and black matching short pajamas set and long red furry socks sipping on a glass of wine watching the news. "Ma, I think I want to have a party here at the house for my birthday. Nothing major, just a few people" "Jahiri, your birthday is in a few weeks I don't think you have time to plan anything like that. I wish you would have said something earlier." "I know, Ma. I just realized that I want to do something. I mean, I usually go all out for my birthday, and this year, I really have a reason to celebrate life, don't you think?" "Yes, well, every day that you wake up with breath in your body, you should be thankful, but I get what you are saying. I just don't think it would be a good idea to have a party this year. I mean, we still have things to think about like your doctor bills and everything." "You know what, Ma, you're right. I don't know what I was thinking." I was in my feeling now, so I went into the room and closed the door, hoping that she wouldn't come busting it open like she used to when I was a kid. I was sick of feeling like I was a kid again in my own home, asking my mother for permission to celebrate my birthday. This is some bullshit. I have to make this proposal work out so I can start creating some extra income, get back on my feet, and have my parents stop helping so much. My mom was right though; I could be taking this time to stack any extra cash that I have to get my savings back in order and invest in any new product that I need to launch my line. I think that is what I want to do as a birthday gift for myself – have my proposal at least ninety percent complete and a few sample items complete. I have made several digital pieces that I will show during my presentation, but it's something about having the actual piece in hand that makes it feel real, at least for me. I have two onesies done, but I really don't like the first one I made; the neckline doesn't seem to be even so I may do that one over. I'm nervous, but my ultimate goal is to get Ms. Kelly to invest in my line of clothes, create a website for ordering, that way, I can focus more on building the brand without the hassle of maintaining an actual building and maybe pitch it to a few established boutiques to see if they would be willing to sell some pieces in the store. My initial mindset was that in order for me to have a business, I need to have a building, but through experience, I am learning that, first, I need to create a great product, and it will sell if I put in the work to market it. Looking at the line I helped Ms. Kelly create, it has profited very well, which I learned from keeping her business journals. This has truly inspired me to focus on creating a brand that I believe instead of focusing on owning a building because eventually, I will get there.

I don't want to go to physical therapy today, but I have to get this over with. It wasn't because I had a minute crush on my doctor's husband, but because I was tired of going, I was ready for them to say we can lose the boot, take away the crutch, and I was up walking normal again. I am almost there, so I will keep working hard to get this off my to-do list. This morning Dr. Mel was not there when I arrived, so I began working with her assistant Dee. She was fresh out of school. I could tell by how eager and excited she was about her work. I liked it though; when I worked with Dee, she always played good music and exuded high energy, which got me pumped to complete those workouts. They had two very different techniques when working with patients. Dee was very professional, but she made it a bit more fun, all while training. Dr. Mel was really serious but also very encouraging in a coach kind of way. Either way, they both had to be doing something right because I was feeling like my old self again, and now I can walk without the crutches. When we finished up for the day, I was informed that my session next week will be held at the new facility that they are opening, which is a few blocks away from this place. I remember Dr. Mel telling me that she is working on opening a bigger facility when we first began working together; I didn't know she meant so soon, but either way, it was cool. I learned that Dr. Mel moved to Atlanta for medical school and fell in love with the city, so she opened her practice here, and she dreams of opening a bigger facility one day. I am happy for her. I sat in the lobby waiting on Chrissy listening to the receptionist have a casual conversation discussing a party that is happening this weekend. I could tell Dr. Mel was out today because everyone is usually very dull, almost robotic when she is around.

I was starving, I hope Chrissy has cooked. She wanted to pick me up today to get me out of the house for a little while. I am so glad she is getting back to herself, hopefully even better than before, so she can recognize when she is having a vulnerable moment and address it proactively. Either way, I am just happy to have my friend back. My mother has moved in and taken over my house by rearranging my things to her likings. I didn't have the energy to put up a fight because earlier today, when I was working, she had the audacity to redecorate my entire kitchen. Now I didn't mind her changing the guest bedroom. I mean, she has been there, and I wanted her to feel at home, but she took that as "change my entire place." I am thinking damn boundaries, Ma, but I wouldn't dare say it; I respected my mother too much to disrespect her, and she is only here because she is trying to help me and to be honest; I have enjoyed her being here not so sure I want her to go back home. But definitely wouldn't mind if she and dad found a place out here. I get a call from Chrissy, so I head outside.

"Hey, Bish!"

"I see you are feeling good today. Where is Kj?"

"He is with Keith. They went over his parent's house so I can hang with you for the day... Jahiri, do you think I would be crazy if I said that I am not ready to return back to work? I mean, I spoke with Keith, and he is really happy with that idea."

"I think if you and your husband are on the same page, why do you care what I think? But if you need to hear me say it, no, I don't think you are crazy."

"Yea, I think I want to take a year off to be with my son and really spend time with my husband. Since we have been married, this is the most that I have been home with him. I mean, I work all over the states, so I am usually only home for one week in a month, and that is not sustainable in our marriage, and I cannot leave KJ like that. So, I am thinking about either finding something local or freelance."

"I think that is good Chrissy, I know Keith is going to be happy he has never said it, but I know he misses you."

"Yep, I need to be closer to my family now. And that also means I will get to see you more too."

"Finally," I wanted to tell Chrissy that I was thinking about moving, but she is going through so much right now that I don't want to add to her stress. I mean, it's not like we cannot talk every day on the phone like we have been. I think it will be the same, but it sounds like she doesn't want that. She wants her family now, but I have to also do what is best for me, and she will understand that. I will just tell her once I truly decide what I am going to do. Besides, it is just an idea.

"Hey, let's go to the mall and find you something cute to wear for your birthday."

"I do not have anything to do for my birthday, so I will not need anything new to wear."

"Oh bish, we are taking you out, me and Keith decided this, so you are going. Mrs. Evelyn is coming too. I texted her this morning."

We get to the mall going to several stores when I finally found the perfect outfit for dinner. Chrissy found several options, and she bought them all. She had some new curves since KJ, so she needed a few new pieces. She loved her new little butt and breast that she gained from pregnancy. Since I met her, she has wanted to gain some weight, and she just barely maintained a little of her pregnancy weight, and it looks damn good on her. Once we finished, we went to all the baby stores to get KJ some things. She even got Keith some things. I forgot how much walking is required when going to the mall with Chrissy. She likes to go into every store, whereas I like to go into only the ones that I think that I will find what I need. I began to walk a little slower, and she got the hint, so we left, found something to eat, and went to her house. Her home is beautiful. I mean, she designed it herself. It was like a fine piece of art. I noticed that she purchased some of the pillows that I designed. She supports me even without me knowing, that's a true friend. KJ has taken over almost every room with all of his toys and baby gadgets. Shortly after we arrived at Chrissy's house, Keith came walking in the door. "Baby, what are you doing here? I thought you and KJ were at your parents." "We are, I forgot to bring him a change of clothes, and he shit all over himself and my mom. HaHa." "Haha, damn, I told you to take extra clothes." "You did baby; you did. I don't know what I would do without you." They began to kiss and feel all over each other. I loved their relationship. They weren't trying to pretend to be the perfect couple, but you could tell that their love for one another was genuine. I would love to go out with my friend and her husband and not be the third wheel, especially now that she has a whole family; I really will feel like I am just in the way. I know they don't mind or at least they don't show that they do. Well, when it happens, it happens. I am in no rush because I want it to be real and just for me. "Oh please, stop it with all that freaky shit; you two are going to mess around and have baby number two." "What's up Jahiri, are you ready for your birthday dinner? It's going to be lit!" Chrissy nudges him. "Yea, I am ready, but you won't be able to turn up like you used to; you're a dad now." "Oh, hell, me and wifey are going to be kid-free, so we are turning up for your birthday even if it is just us, you know how we do, haha." He is right, those two know how to party, and I mean party even if it is just the two of them. Once we all went out to this party where it was dead, I mean, everyone sitting, talking, and drinking, yet they were the only fools on the dance floor jumping around like they were a live concert. It was hilarious, I mean I would have gotten out there, but it was much more fun laughing at them. Keith finally decides to get what he came for, which truthfully was his game. We already knew his parent basically had an entire bedroom of clothes for their first grandson.

Chapter 23: White Coat

I cannot believe that my birthday is so close; I am actually excited. This is the one time that I really try to think about myself by doing exactly what makes me feel good. I am not sure what I will be doing this year, but I am still excited. I completed physical therapy with Dr. Mel for today, but she left about twenty minutes before I was finished. I don't know what the urgency was about, but she left in a hurry. Her new office is so beautiful. I mean, you can tell that she took her time with this place. I know her prices are going to skyrocket with all of the services she provides. Apparently, she has a new doctor that she is partnering with, which is why she has gotten a bigger place so that they can take more patients. They have a beautiful seating area outside that I was excited to check out, so I brought my proposal and sketchbook so that I could sit and relax after therapy today. Dr. Mel gave me the okay saying, that is why they built it for their patients to have a relaxing and calming place to enjoy before or after therapy.

I didn't have anything planned today actually nothing at all this week until my birthday Saturday. I have been debating on how I can ask Ms. Kelly if I could pitch her my work but I haven't gathered the courage to send her the email. I mean the worst she could say is no and I am used to hearing that. I think I just don't want that feeling right now right before my birthday; I have been sad enough this year I just want this one day to be happy. "So, did you fall today or just decided to take a seat?" I look up, and it is Landon who is dressed like he is heading to or coming from the gym. "Oh, today, I actually decided to sit on the ground this time." "What is that you are working on?" I am trying not to engage in conversation with him. I don't want people to think that I am trying to flirt with Dr. Mel's husband. "Oh, just some sketches." "Sketches of what?" I look up at him because he apparently doesn't recognize that I am being short and not trying to have this conversation with him. "I'm sorry…" Before I could finish, Dr. Mel pops up out of nowhere, and her youngest daughter runs up to where we are. "Hey, Uncle Landon, guess what? I forgot my permission slip, so I wasn't able to go on my field trip today, so I get to hang up here with you and mom." They fist pump as Dr. Mel walks up "don't encourage her bad behavior. She left it at home on purpose. Ms. Strong, you really decided to take a break out here. It's peaceful, isn't it?" "It sure is." "Sooo Landon, this is the young lady that you have been bugging me about, huh?" "She is beautiful, Uncle Landon, I think you should ask her out already." I feel so stupid. Instead of just asking him, I assumed that he was her husband when he is her brother. "You don't officially work here yet, bro, so I will give you a pass besides I like Ms. Strong, and I would love to have her as a sister-in-law." She winks at me, grabs her daughter, and head into the office. "So, you have been looking for me?" "Well…yea I wanted to talk to you more that day, but your mom came, and you looked as though you were having a bad day. Then when I saw you during family day, you left so quickly that I couldn't approach you." "I am going to be blunt with you. I was hoping to see you again too, but when I finally did, you were with Dr. Mel and her kids. I assumed you were her husband." "Haha, her what? Wow, that's crazy. That's my oldest sister, who thinks she is my mom well, she is like my mom she helped raise me, so we are very close. I am in the process of moving to Atlanta. I graduate next month with my white coat, so I will be her new partner here. Her husband, hahaha, that's still funny." "Congratulations, that is awesome." He sits down next to me, asking if he could look at my sketches, and surprisingly, I pass it to him. "I am sorry before I go on, I really need to ask you…what is your first name? My sister would not give it to me." I smile, "my name is Jahiri." He stares me in the eyes for a second with a smile on his face then holds up the sketchbook. "These are really nice sketches, Jahiri Strong; I would love to find out more about them and you." "Oh, really, how do you suggest we do that?" "Well, it would be an honor if you allow me take you out." "Honor, huh? I think we can do that." I give him my number, and we make plans for later tomorrow.

On the ride home, my mom was talking, but I was in lala land. I have never had a guy show so much interest in me. I mean, looking for me and asking his sister to introduce us, I think it is cute. He sat and talked with me the entire hour that I was waiting outside for my mom to come. He is a really cool guy. I mean, he is gorgeous but also very intelligent, easy to talk to, and he loves his family. I learned that his sister raised him after their parents passed, which is why they are so close. It's something about him that I am interested in knowing more. The conversation was just amazing. We decided to go to dinner and then the arcade. For some reason, I am not nervous; I am actually excited about our date.

The next morning after I finish my work out, I receive a call from Landon. "Good Morning Jahiri, how are you today?" "Good Morning, I am doing well. How about you?" "I am great. I thought about you, so I wanted to call and say hello and make sure we are on for today." "Sweet, and yes, of course, we are." "Well, I actually have to go looking at a few apartments. If you aren't busy right now, you are welcomed to join me." "Sure!" Damn, did I sound too excited? I hope he doesn't think I am a bomb who doesn't have anything to do. I mean I really don't Ms. Kelly gave me the week off because she had an event this week and she has hired a new assistant, so I only really check over her assistant work for now and so far, she is doing really good. "Great, I can pick you up in about an hour if that works." "I will be ready." I hurry to get dressed and comb my hair, which resulted in jeans, t-shirt, and ponytail. I decided to put a little makeup and lip gloss nothing to much he needs to know who I truly am and I am simple until I feel like being over the top. When Landon arrives, my mom invites him in because I was still trying to get dressed. I really have butterflies. I know that I have on something basic, but I want to be presentable. I mean, he has only ever seen me at physical therapy, so I get a pass for how I dress there. When I walk out there, he stands up to greet me. He has on jean shorts and white t-shirt. "Look at you two already dressing alike, so cute." I sigh at my mom for making this awkward as I grab my purse and walk out the door.

"You know what is so cool about our situation?" "What?" "I have already met your mom, and you have met my sister and nieces so that pressure of meeting the family is not really there." "Well, you haven't met my entire family. I mean, my dad and older sister Eve, they are two to meet." "Oh, I plan on meeting them too." "So, you plan on being around that long, huh?" "If you allow me to." We ride around and look at three apartments, none of which he was in love with. We ended up spending the entire day together, and I enjoyed every minute of it. I told him my plans for the sketches, and he somehow talked me into sending the email to Ms. Kelly while we were waiting for our food. I sent it but I didn't check my email for a response just because I didn't want to know if she said no. I was happy to have done it though it felt good to put myself out there again in an attempt to work on my goal.

For the rest of the week, Landon and I talked every day; we even hung out when he wasn't at the office getting things together. He would be working there once he actually graduates; he is excited about it and very passionate about it. He told me that mostly through medical school, his sister covered most of his bills. He didn't like it, but now he appreciates it because it helped him reach his ultimate goal of becoming a doctor. I love how supportive his sister is of him as he is of her. Their bond is beautiful. I invited him to attend my birthday dinner with Chrissy and Keith, but he already had prior engagements so he wouldn't be able to make it. I wasn't upset because it was very short notice. My mother, for some reason, decided that of all time, she wanted to go home on my birthday weekend so she wouldn't be here to celebrate, but I wasn't upset. I am in a happy place and tomorrow is my birthday, so I am going to make the best of it.

Chapter 24: It's a Birthday Celebration

I wake up to several text messages and missed phone calls. I sit up in my bed and listen to each of them. Chrissy tried to get me for the full day, but I just wanted to do something by myself, so I did. I got up, got dressed, called for a car, and went to breakfast. I have never minded doing things on my own, and today was no different; I sat at the table and enjoyed my breakfast with a very delicious mimosa. Afterward, I decided to go to the nail salon, which was much needed and very relaxing. As I was sitting there getting my toes polished even the foot with the ugly boot, I received an email alert. It was from Ms. Kelly. I sat for a second deciding if I was going to open it when I realized that either way, I was still going to get my clothing line out I just may have to look for different investors. So, I removed the fear of receiving a no response by channeling positive solution-driven outcomes realizing that I only become a failure if I give up if she decides against it. I opened it, and my heart dropped. She sent an email accepting my request to hear my proposal, also sending three calendar invites to choose from for next week to present. I chose the second one for Wednesday at 10:00 a.m. I thought I was on cloud nine before well, I was having the best fucking birthday ever.

When I made it home, I had about four hours before I had to be ready for Chrissy, which meant I really had about three. I didn't have anything to do, so I went to the bathroom to start combing my hair. I think I am going to straighten it. I search for my flat irons that I barely use, which is why it is always so hard to find. Then I see the boxes of copper hair dye I purchased a while back. Before I knew it, I am sitting in my bathroom with copper dye all over my head and I start to notice it change colors, then the nerves kicked in. Oh shit, what have I done?? I am going to look like a complete fool. If Eve were here, she would say what were you thinking doing that goofy-ass shit? Fuck it; it's done who cares what anyone else thinks. When I washed my hair, I stand in front of the mirror; about fifteen minutes of just staring at myself, I started to really like it. I haven't done anything this impulsive since I cut all my hair off, but I am actually loving this color on me. I decided to do a wash in go instead just to see how my curls are going to look with this beautiful copper color against my brown skin. While sitting under the dryer I receive a message from Sabrina who must have gotten my number from my dad as well. It said…Happy Birthday, Jahiri I hope you are having an amazing one, love you even if you don't believe it. I was in a good mood, so I sent her a text back, thanks. I saw the bubbles pop up, but she never said anything else. I know she and I will never be friends the way we were again, but I did not have the energy to hold a grudge, so my replying was simply my way of letting her know that I forgive her, and I think she understands.

I am finally dressed in my distressed fitted jeans, cream crop top and beautiful oversized peach blazer that I found when shopping with Chrissy. I would wear heels with this, but one cute sandal is going to work just fine. "Oh shit, you look good girl that boot not stopping shit today bish! And this color is absolutely gorgeous on you!" "Thank you, girl, where is Keith?" "We didn't have a sitter, so it is just the two of us." "Cool," I was actually happy I really didn't feel like being their third wheel for my birthday this year. As we ride to the restaurant, I almost slip up and tell Chrissy about my meeting with Ms. Kelly, but she didn't even know that I was working on this line, so I kept it to myself. Not that she wouldn't support me, it's just something that I want to keep to myself for a little while longer. We pass the restaurant that I was told we're going to, but I guess since it is just us, she changed plans, so I didn't even bring it up. We finally pull up to this beautiful venue. "Hey this is one of the places that I help designed, and the owner gave me a discounted rate for a nice dinner here." "Oh, that's so nice of you, Chrissy" I was pinching on her cheeks and trying to give her a hug. "Oh, just get your ass out of the car." We walk in, and this place does not look close to a restaurant; it looks more so like an event space but beautiful, to say the least I mean, she designed it so I wouldn't expect anything less. We walk down this long hall and finally get to these double doors when I open it up; I almost pissed my pants "SURPRISE" I mean everyone that I could think of was there my parents, Eve, some other friends and family. I even saw Sasha, who now lives in Texas with her husband and kids, which is why I don't get to see her as much. I was so surprised that they pulled this off. I mean, I had no clue. I turned to thank Chrissy, but she told me this was all Eve's doing. She was just the assistant. I was in utter shock. I found Eve to give her a hug, and I believe I thanked her a thousand times. Today was truly amazing. I get out on the dance floor dancing and just having a good time until the DJ took it upon himself to put on a slow jam, so I took myself over to the table to get some food when I get a tap on my shoulder. "Landon, wait now how did you find out about all of this?" "Your mother invited me the day I came to pick you up, is it okay that I am here?" "I am happy that you are here." "Wow, I love this color on you, you look amazing Jahiri." "Thank you." We eat, mingle, and dance all night. This birthday has truly been one to remember.

Later that night, Landon and I were sitting at the table when I told him that Ms. Kelly wants to hear my pitch. He was happy for me and even offered to help me with my presentation since I told him how I hated public speaking. I don't know why I felt so comfortable sharing all of this information with him; it's like he is getting the grown mature Jahiri, where I am raw, open, and honest with who I am and my aspirations, but he accepts it; I really appreciate having someone in my corner. I mean, he doesn't hold back his opinion, but if we differ, he doesn't make me feel like my process is wrong. I also like that he doesn't just find a way to criticize without trying to help find a better solution. I wish my family more so Eve were like that. I just began to realize that all of my life that I have been seeking the approval of Eve when in actuality, I never needed her approval from the beginning.

He and I were not a couple yet, but I saw the potential for a meaningful relationship. He and I just seemed to have an instant bond. It just feels real. Chrissy and Keith come up to me while I was taking a break from dancing when I hear Keith, "Sis, he passed the test, so we welcome Landon into our lives." "Yea, we like him. Not only is he intelligent, but he knows how to have a good time, and I have never seen a guy make you smile this much since I have known you, Jahiri. I hope he is around for a while." "Well, thank you both for your approval." I don't know why they think they have that much influence over my life, but I am glad they like him. My sister just loves him because he is a doctor, and my parents like the fact that he makes me smile. I am not rushing into anything serious since it is so new, but to be completely honest, I am not opposed to the idea of being in a relationship with him. He and I just seemed to have an instant bond like a true friendship. I like that he challenges me to make moves instead of waiting for the perfect time. I also like that he accepts me for simply being myself, and I am actually learning to love the woman that I am becoming. I never thought that I would be here today, but through it all, I am glad that I have had this experience. It has taught me that I can make it through tough times, and this past year has been one tough year. I am excited to see what twenty-seven has to offer.

The next day, my family, Chrissy, Keith, Keith's parents, and Chrissy's dad all decided to go out for brunch. "So Jahiri, you are almost ready to get back to your normal life, what are your plans? Do you have any jobs lined up?" "I actually do not have anything at the moment, Eve, but I am working on a few things." "I hope it is not that design mess. You should come home and help Momma run the daycare. I mean, you do have a business degree, help her franchise it." "She doesn't want to run a daycare, Eve, and besides, I am preparing to retire. I don't want to open any more daycares." "Well, if she would just come back home, then you would be able to retire knowing that she is up there, making sure it is running a float; besides, you cannot stay down here forever, taking care of her." "Look, Eve, I honestly don't understand why you are always so opinionated when it comes to my life, but you are right, Ma can't stay here forever to HELP me. In fact, I am not moving back home. I am working on a children's clothing line that has a really great potential to be a success. Before you say anything, I don't need nor want your opinion on what I am doing in my life because it is my life." As I get up from the table, I see Chrissy smiling, giving me the nod like "about damn time." I walk outside to keep from saying anything else because I really wanted to hit below the belt, but what would that have proven besides hurting her the way she has been trying to hurt me my entire life. I thought things were getting better between us, but since her ex-husband has had his new baby, she has been tripping. And that new boyfriend of hers was just a phase of hers to avoid addressing her true feelings with the divorce. Why does she always take her hurt and anger out on the people who love her the most? I will never understand. The restaurant door swings open, "I don't know why you let her get you so worked up, you know she only does it to get a reaction out of you." "I know daddy, but she acts like I am still a kid. I mean, sometimes she goes harder on me than she is on her own kids. I am just tired of it; I just don't understand why she hates me so much." "Jahiri, you know that your sister doesn't hate you. In fact, she begged your mother and I for a sister her whole life, but we were so consumed with work trying to create a better life for her that we lost sight of having another child. Well, when your mother found out she was pregnant, it did come as a bit of a surprise, but we were happy. Your sister was happy even though she was almost grown. She just wanted to have a sibling. After you were born, your mother's daycare was running well, and I was doing fairly well, and we were more financially stable from when we had Eve, so we were able to do more for you. We spoiled you as she would say, whereas we did give her a little more tough love because we wanted her to know that life would not be easy, and she would have to work harder than most. We tried with you, but we were much older, and times were different, so I guess she took it upon herself to be that tough love you needed so that you would have some fight in you. If you ask me, she did a good job. I just wish we didn't make her feel as though that was her responsibility." "I didn't know that daddy. I never thought about how our childhood could have differed. I assumed that it was the same since we had the same parents, but I never asked. I mean, she was out of the house by the time I could remember anything. I know Eve loves me; I just hate that she uses her words to hurt instead of encourage sometimes. I guess it is because I am older now I want her to respect me for the woman I am today not just looking at me through the lenses of being just her baby sister." "You have every right to feel that way. Just give her some time, she has a tough exterior, but she is soft as a marsh mellow on the inside. She will come around and talk to you." "Thanks, daddy."

"Come on, are you two ready? Zachariah is the table showing out, my daughters are arguing; I am just over this brunch. Come on, baby, let's go with Keith's parents. They want to take us to this museum."

My mom has changed a lot over the years, she has always been tough, but the older I got, the nicer she became, and now that she is preparing to retire, she is really focusing on being happy, and I get it. Keith comes out talking mess with Zachariah while Chrissy is holding KJ looking as though she isn't prepared for him to turn his age. I just laugh because my nephew is a little monster when he wants to be.

Chapter 25: If Tears had a Voice

My family will be leaving tomorrow night; including my mom. She finally feels comfortable leaving me. I have to admit I will miss her being around so much. She and my father have made plans to come back and visit more since they both will be retired. I love the thought of that; hopefully, things work out well so that I can finally do something special for them for once. Something big, I have always desired to do well in life so that I could return the favor to my parents and even my mean ass sister, Eve. Eve hasn't said anything to me since our argument at the table, I would say I am fine with that, but I am not; however, I don't want to be the one to say I am sorry first because I am not this time. I really meant what I said, and I think it is time that she hears me for a change. I wasn't too concerned about that right now, I have my presentation to think about, and I need it to be the best work that I have done thus far. I keep telling myself that I will not be nervous; I will not stumble over my words. I asked Dr. Mel if I could do my presentation on her a few therapy sessions ago prior to me finding out who Landon was to her, and she eagerly agreed to listen whenever I was ready. Well, I did it for her this morning before my session, and in true Jahiri fashion, I stumbled a little in the beginning. Dr. Mel has that serious, stern look that makes me even more nervous, so I am glad that I did get this practice in. She gave me great feedback, letting me know that everything sounds great, so not to worry. She thinks my proposal is very well written seems to be a good investment. She gave me the contact information to one of her friends who likes to invest in small business just in case Ms. Kelly is unable to at this time. I don't know why things are starting to look so bright for me, but it is making a girl feel really good about myself. I have a new sense of confidence in myself that I never knew that I had. New age, new hair color, overcoming obstacles, taking risks, choosing victory over fear…just all around feeling like a new woman.

I pull up at the house after physical therapy and Eve is sitting outside my house. I don't know why when my mom has the key. I guess she is mad; I bet she is trying to prove a point that I am grown so that's why she didn't go into my house while I wasn't there. Ugh, she is so extra with her ugly self. "Hey, Jahiri, Momma and Dad were downtown somewhere, so I wasn't able to get the key from them before they left. That's why I am sitting out here looking crazy, and it is hot as hell in this Georgia heat." Damn, was she reading my mind? I guess I was wrong. "Oh, you're cool, I thought maybe Ma locked herself out or something." That was a straight lie. "Now you know damn well she is not going to let that happen, haha. Hurry up and let me in the house I have to get out of this damn heat my edges are sweating; this hair due has to last me until my next salon appointment this weekend." Look at her acting as if we didn't have an argument the other day. It's cool I can keep pretending right along with her. "You want some water?" "Yes, none of that faucet water though; I'll take a bottle of water if you have any." "Here you go." "Look, I am going to get straight to it. I heard you the other day, and you are right. Funny thing is…I have always believed in you; I just felt like you didn't believe in yourself. I mean, when you got your first job out of college, you hated it, but I didn't understand why you even took it when you had the intern. Then, you applied for business loans, and when they told you no a few times, you just gave up. I mean, starting anything is going to be hard, but you cannot give up, and that's what I don't like. I think our parents spoiled you, and you don't like to hear no, but I want you to realize that life isn't easy, that's why I am always on your case. I think you are a phenomenal designer, intelligent, focused, hardworking yet hard-headed, and very independent. However, you like to play it safe, and sometimes you give up on yourself. You are young. This is your time to mess up and figure things out. You just cannot get complacent because that is when you get stuck in a never ending cycle of unsustainability." As I am sitting here listing to my sister, a tear forms in my eye, but I hold it in. "Look, you are right. You don't need my opinion on your life. I have just been trying to pull out of you what it is you really want to do. I mean, you worked a job that you hated until they let you go. How long will you have stayed there had they not only because it was paying the bills?" She is right, I may have still been tiring myself out for a job that I hated, and I wouldn't be working on this clothing line for sure. I hate to admit it, but she has some valid points. There was complete silence for about a minute. "Eve, have you ever walked in the shadows of someone who has accomplished so much? I mean, our parents bragged about you my entire life, and I admired you. I was always so happy to say my sister, the Doctor. When I told you and our parents that I wanted to be a designer, the reactions that I got from you all made me feel that it wasn't enough like it didn't measure up to your expectations. I felt like it wasn't good enough, meaning that I wasn't good enough, so yea, I figured if I made more money and had a title that you all would respect me more. Then when things really fell apart, I felt like you all were right. I was ashamed. I have always only been seeking your approval and acceptance, but over the course of the year, I have learned to accept that I am not you, and that is okay." "Oh shit, you are going to make me mess up my make up. We accept, approve, and love everything about you. Don't you ever; I mean ever question that again no matter how much shit I talk." We both began to laugh, wiping the tears from our faces. Eve reaches over to gives me a hug, then reaches in her purse and passes me an envelope requesting that I not open it until after I complete my presentation. We sat and talked for a minute longer until our dad came busting through the door with the boys. They claimed they had to go to the restroom, so my parent turned around. Eve and I decided to make it a family day, so we went with them downtown and even persuaded our parents to get on the Ferris wheel, which was hilarious.

It is finally the day, and to say that I am nervous would be an understatement right now. Ms. Kelly just came to let me know they will be ready for me in five minutes. I didn't even know there would be other people here now. I am really going insane. I am so glad Chrissy suggested that I wear this black dress suit today because I know for a fact that my armpits are sweaty right now. "Ms. Strong, they are ready for you in the conference room A." I have so many thoughts running through my head right now. "You can do this," I continue to say over and over in my head. When I get to the room, there are ten women, including Ms. Kelly, all sitting in a row looking quite solemn and focused. I finally get to the front of the room, introduce myself, and there it was the tremble in my voice that I know they hear as well. I take a quick pause, gather my thoughts, take a deep breath, and proceed. I find Ms. Kelly among the women in the room because I know her, and she gave me a sense of comfort. In the midst of me sharing my designs and business model, I notice the lady two seats from Ms. Kelly smiling, so I began to look at her. By the end of the presentation, I forgot that I was ever nervous; it's like I felt confident in myself being the lead for a change, and it felt good. In my opinion, this was the best presentation that I have ever done.

After the presentation, I go back out in the sitting area, which is really more so the break room and wait for about twenty minutes before I am called back in the room. There is a woman who stands up shakes my hand as she introduces herself and let me know that she works with Ms. Kelly to help develop and sponsor young upcoming entrepreneurs; a program that they started over ten years ago to give back to the community by mentoring and sponsoring aspiring young women who have a great business plan. "We have been hearing about you for years, and it is so good to finally meet you. Sasha spoke highly of you, so we knew that you had to be an amazing young lady because she is a tough one to break." I was sitting there astonished thinking, is this why she got me this job after graduation. Did I miss an opportunity? The woman interrupted my thoughts. "Well, we love your work; it reflects that it was well thought out, very thorough in the budget, exhibits some great and unique pieces that will be profitable. I am saying this all to say that we would love to help you execute your vision, Ms. Strong. Congratulations."

I was sitting in a room full of women who had never met me but showed more excitement in my dream more than some people I have known my entire life. It truly felt amazing. I cannot describe the emotion that I am feeling right now; it is beyond ecstatic, grateful, joyful, it is just something I cannot describe. Before I left the room from speaking with each of the ladies; Ms. Kelly pulled me to the side and gave me what I consider a gift because I did not expect it, nor did I request a store location within my proposal. I walked into the meeting just taking a chance on myself with no real expectations; however, I walked out being offered help in developing my line, and Ms. Kelly offered her store for rent at a very, very discounted rate for the next two years. I wasn't thinking of the fact that I didn't have enough to rent the space for two years; I am more so soaking in gratitude for having so many offers on the table. I am in disbelief that I came in requesting for help to develop my clothing line, and I was walking out with that and more.

I couldn't make it to my car, so I sat on the stairs in the stairway because my emotions were at an all-time high. I cried thanking God for giving me this year, granting me the opportunity to work on myself and executing all of the things that I had put to the side. After about fifteen minutes I got myself together finally containing my excitement and joy As I was preparing to leave, Eve's card fell out of my portfolio. I was just about to stuff it back into my bag, but something made me open it. Inside was a check and a note that read

...Someone helped me, so I want to help you-Happy Birthday.

Throughout this year, I have been questioning every tear that derived from sadness, hurt, anger, fear, frustration, pity, doubt, uncertainty, and more, but now I understand that every tear served its purpose. And as I sit here with more falling from my eyes deriving from relief, happiness, clarification, and joy, I understand how it all has prepared me for this moment and the journey to come.

www.ingramcontent.com/pod-product-compliance
Lightning Source LLC
Chambersburg PA
CBHW072009170626
46813CB00005B/2079